OCCUPATIONAL
HAZARD

OCCUPATIONAL HAZARD

An Al and Mick Forte Story

ALEX S. AVITABILE

Occupational Hazard

This is a work of fiction and is the product of the author's imagination.
People, places and things mentioned are all fictitious. Any resemblance
to actual persons, living or dead, is entirely coincidental.

For information about this title, contact
Alex S. Avitabile either via the contact page of the
www.AlandMickForte.net website
or by emailing alex@AlandMickForte.net.

Library of Congress Control Number: 2018905870

ISBN Trade Paperback: 978-1-7323063-0-1

ISBN eBook: 978-1-7323063-1-8

Printed in the United States of America

Cover and Interior design: 1106 Design

Author Photo by Ron Jordan Natoli and Steve Warham of Ron
Jordan Natoli Studio, 352 Court Street, Brooklyn, NY 11231

This book is dedicated to my beloved late wife

THERESA LIU-AVITABILE

who is surely as surprised as I that
I was able to finish writing it.

CONTENTS

CHAPTER 1

"Ciao, Baby!"

"YOU'RE OUT!" GORDON Gilbert bellows as I sit down.

I'm out? What is this asshole talking about? Could he be referring to that play at the firm's picnic where he pretended that he hadn't dropped the ball while trying to tag me. One of the other partners had to mediate the call, and I was declared safe at third, having legged out a nifty triple.

But he couldn't, he wouldn't, be referring to that play.

Annual reviews at the law firm of Gilbert & Associates, PLLP happen during the late summer/early autumn, always unannounced, despite the countless management team firm-wide e-mails and its blog. G&A, as we referred to the firm (note the absence of "affectionately" in that phrase), was a law firm of some 350 attorneys, distributed about in the five offices G&A maintained across the U.S. Most of us were at its headquarters here in New York City, where I was employed, when I was summoned to Gordon Gilbert's office on the Wednesday after Labor Day.

G&A started about twelve years ago as a thirty-attorney real estate boutique, founded by Gordon Gilbert, Joan Zakorski, and two other attorneys who are no longer with the firm. These four lawyers left the real estate department of a prestigious Wall Street firm to create a law practice where they alone could decide how it is run, whom it services and, perhaps most importantly, how the firm's collections are divided.

The acknowledged leader of the four is Gilbert, a brilliant attorney with no equal in analytical skills and a great understanding of all aspects of real estate law and practice. Gilbert is a shrewd, cutthroat negotiator who can be outgoing and affable when he wants to be but, deep down, is egotistical, bombastic, and power-hungry. He is someone who has no patience for disagreement and who takes no prisoners.

All these attributes contributed to Gilbert's ability to build a national firm of exceptional prominence, by raiding other firms of their rainmakers and merging with top firms in strategically located markets across the U.S. The acknowledged leader of this much larger, diverse firm remained Gilbert. Among the heavy hitters, Gilbert was a home run hitter. Among the rainmakers, he created torrents, while the others made it drizzle.

And Gilbert's power was not limited to G&A. He was held in high esteem in the larger legal community and wielded vast influence with local and national bar associations. His legal prowess attracted significant clients with ongoing projects that kept G&A partners and associates humming virtually around the clock, and which put Gilbert in a position of influence with the major players. All of which made him a power broker not only within the private sector but in the public sector as well. Politicians and wanna-be politicians sought his support. He had a say in who would be nominated for elected positions and who would get governmental agency appointments, including the selection of judges.

At G&A's headquarters, annual reviews became known as associates were quietly marshaled, one at a time, into Gilbert's office where each one was grilled and chastised by Gilbert and several other partners. Each associate walked out ashen-faced and with drooping shoulders, having been knocked around, mostly by Gilbert. Luckily, compensation for the following calendar year was not at issue at these sessions. Luckier still, compensation decisions were determined by the Human Resources Committee, from which Gilbert was intentionally excluded. To quell a partner revolt against his dictatorial powers a few years back, it was decided that three partners, none named Gordon Gilbert, would oversee HR matters. However, to appease Gilbert, he was given the last say on hiring and the first say on firing. Nevertheless, as partners allied with (and beholden to) Gilbert relinquished what little power they had, Gilbert's power base was in fact strengthened.

As I sit there that fateful Wednesday, Gilbert is in the process of exercising the first-say power vested in him.

"You're out!" he repeats and then adds, "You must be out of here by two weeks from this Friday. That means that all work presently pending must be satisfactorily completed, all the firm's files in your possession properly organized, an appropriate exit memo drafted and signed off on by your supervising partner, and all of your personal crap packed up and removed from the premises."

"I'm fired?" I inquire.

"Yes. You are fired, let go, terminated, however you want to put it. Banished!" Gilbert shouts.

"Can you give me a clue why? I wasn't aware that my work was unsatisfactory."

"You want to know why? I will tell you why," Gilbert says. "Because you are a candy-ass pansy and I do not like you and your liberal ways. 'Fair this,' 'equity that,' 'inequality' here, there and everywhere. You put all this nonsense into the heads of the other associates. You are a terrible influence on them and I can't stand to have you here any longer. You can't seem to get into that thick wop skull of yours that fair is what I say is fair and is in our clients' best interests."

The other partners blanch a bit on the mention of "wop," but I let it slide.

"I'm only aware of clients being satisfied with my work," I say.

"That's because the only clients we give you face time with are those do-gooders, the nonprofits or the for-profit fools, involved in the development of affordable housing. Luckily, there's a few bucks to be made in those deals. I've decided I no longer want you to take up any of my space. Besides, you're not G&A partner material."

After about seven years of practice, attorneys at firms are either elevated to partner or let go. I had worked several years for a small firm before making a lateral move to G&A.

"I'm sorry you feel that way."

"Fuck you, sorry. Just get your shit together and make sure you are out of here in two weeks and two days. And if you fail to fully comply with the terms I outlined, you'll be docked whatever remaining pay you're otherwise owed."

"How about severance?" I state more than ask, as I know that is firm policy.

"Severance? You're not getting shit!"

"Excuse me, Gordon, but severance is a decision within the domain of the HR Committee and Al will need to take it up with them," wimp of a partner, Joe Baker, meekly states.

"Whatever. I'm just glad that I need to be out of town the next ten days or so and won't have to see this asshole's face more than a few more times."

"Fuck you," I blurt out uncontrollably under my breath.

"What did you just say?"

"Nothing," I respond.

"Well, if you really didn't say anything, I know you thought 'Fuck you.' Well, all I have left to say is: *Ciao*, baby! —and a very good riddance."

CHAPTER 2

"Pray our paths never cross again!"

I'M MAKING THE rounds bidding good-byes to my soon-to-be-former colleagues. As I'm chatting with the evening receptionist, Mary Woodley, Gilbert walks through the reception area to go to the men's room and Mary informs him that his son had called.

Gilbert's eyes widen and he shouts: "I just return from being out of town for ten days and you tell my son that I'm too busy to talk to him?"

Mary replies, "But they told me you were meeting with Mr. Guttmann and I figured you did not want to be disturbed."

Gilbert screams at Mary, "You fucking idiot," as he storms over to the waiting area phone. Apparently, he dials his son and gets voice mail, for he then yanks the phone, cord and all, and flings it across the reception area where it smashes into a vase creating a mess of flowers, water, and pieces of crystal.

"Gordon, get a grip! Mary thought she was to hold your calls while you were in your meeting."

"Forte, get out of my face. And why the fuck are you here? You don't work here anymore." Gilbert then remembers, "Oh, yeah, today's your last day."

Turning his attention to junior partner Robert Keenan, who happens to be passing by, he says, "Keenan, if this *putz* Forte isn't out of here by 6:30 sharp, call building security and tell them we have a trespasser here. Tell them that I insist that they hold Forte until the police arrive to take him into custody."

Fortunately, the office manager, Rosa Ortiz, appears and takes over. Rosa is one of the few persons at the firm who can control Gilbert, reportedly due to their "secret" affair that everyone seems to know about. "Gordon, I'm working with Al on his move and it's all good. And let me handle the situation with Mary and get this mess you made cleaned up. Get back to Guttmann; Joan's holding him at bay. Guttman's even more impatient than you, if that's possible. And by the way, your son called me after he spoke to Mary. I told him that you were at a meeting with an important client. All he wants to know is whether you returned, because he needs some cash. So, everything is under control. Except you. So, relax."

With that, Gilbert harrumphs, looks at me and says, "Pray our paths never cross again!" He then heads back into his office to continue with his meeting with Herbert Guttmann, one of the firm's more important clients.

This is the climax to my five-year stint at Gilbert & Associates, PLLP. And it caps off the last couple of weeks of hellacious activity, during which I worked sixteen hours daily, including weekends, to wrap up all my work. The most important task is an analysis of the zoning ordinance *vis-à-vis* a client's proposed development of a vacant parcel of land acquired at a high price. Long story short: The proposed development would not be permitted under the ordinance or under any of its variance rules. My final review of the draft memo, prepared by a junior associate under my supervision, isn't concluded until the early hours of the morning of my last day.

Although I do wrap everything up on time, Gilbert docks me a week's pay. He's not satisfied with the conclusion of the zoning memo, even though the partner who oversaw that assignment signed off on it. Fortunately, since compensation decisions are the exclusive domain of the firm's HR Committee, my appeal is eventually upheld—though it takes two months for me to be paid what had been docked. And it takes the firm another three months before I am paid the severance due me. While Gilbert had no say in the matter, I am sure those payments were delayed to appease him.

CHAPTER 3

"Sounds like a sensible plan."

"HOW'D YOUR WIFE take the news of you gettin' fired," my cousin Mick asks.

"I really didn't tell her," I say.

"Whatdya mean, you didn't really tell her. She knows, don't she? You ain't been goin' to work for coupla months now."

"I didn't have to tell her, she read it in my face."

"Oh, that Theresa. If only you were half as sharp as her."

My wife Theresa and Mick were kindred spirits. Both are very much alike, being blessed with rare common sense, astute judgment and confidence—and toughness and fear-lessness too. She always beseeched me to learn from Mick's "street smarts," as she, like him, felt that formal education had serious shortcomings unless and until informed by practical experience. She urged me to confer with Mick, to listen to him to get the benefit of his view of things and to never look askance at his suggestions.

Our different views of Mick were a source of occa-sional contention. I would pooh-pooh some of her conclu-sions about Mick's success. Theresa would complain that I was being defensive and jealous because Mick was so successful without the education I had. I vehemently dis-agreed with that assessment. While I certainly did have generally positive feelings about my cousin, I thought he jumped to conclusions, could be rash and would frequently plunge into things without thinking them through. Mick, like Theresa, saw things as being black and white, while I found things to have the shade of gray and complicated. Theresa argued that they were simply able to cut to the quick and exclude irrelevant considerations, whereas I would wallow around considering unimportant aspects of situations that demanded action.

Mick was fully aware that he had an ally in Theresa and he tapped that allegiance as a resource in situations such as the matter at hand.

Mick continued, "How'd she take it?"

"She was fabulous. In fact, she was happy I'm free of Gilbert and says she will support whatever I decide to do. Whatever firm I decide to go with—assuming I get an offer—or if I decide to go it alone."

"That's great. How's the job search?"

"Terrible, to tell you the truth. I know I'm a good lawyer and did top-notch work at G&A, but not a bite from any firms and the headhunters can't explain why."

"You think that scumbag Gilbert got anythin' to do with it?"

"Sounds like it. A couple of other associates were let go too, neither anywhere near as qualified as I am, and they got placed quickly. One told me there were senior associate openings at her new firm, but when the headhunter sent over my resume, the reply was unusually prompt and blunt, 'Thanks, but no thanks.' When the headhunter pushed, the hiring partner said that it was out of her hands, that the senior partner there quashed it."

"Gotta be that fuck Gilbert's tryin' to screw you. Well, I figured somethin' like this was happenin' since you still don't got no job. I got some suggestions for you, if you care to lower yourself to consider suggestions from someone as illiterate as your cuz here."

"Now, Mick, please don't start! I'm stressed enough as it is."

"Okay, then just listen. I already talked about this with Theresa and she says she's gonna kick your ass if you don't listen good to what I say."

"Okay, shoot—and I don't mean that literally—in case you're carrying."

"Hey. I never carried, so don't insult me."

"Sorry, sorry. Go on. What's your suggestion?"

"Since your job search's down the toilet, you gonna need to open your own office. I know you don't want nuttin' to do with me, 'cause you think I'm a hood and all."

"Hold it right there, Mick. I know your days in the so-called life are mostly in the past, that you are now mostly legit, so don't tell me what I think. Please."

"Okay, that's good to hear. Anyways, my businesses got to where I gotta deal with all the bullshit rigmarole that all youse straights gotta do. You know, payroll, deductions, taxes, benefits, yada yada yada. The whole shebang. Joe Cohen, that accountant you set me up with, has helped me with all that crap. Lots. I even talked with him about what I'm thinkin' about for you, and he ain't got no problem with it and says he's gonna make sure it all gets done right."

"Look, Mick, as a lawyer, I have to maintain my independence."

"I knows all that, but you ain't heard squat yet. So, *sta zitt* and listen for a change. First, you gotta have clients. I could use an attorney to call on and get on the phone without playin' ring-around-the-rosey. So, I'd wantcha to be my—whatcha call it? —in-house attorney, that's it. You be on my payroll."

"Wait, Mick, you wouldn't have enough work to keep me busy full-time. Nor would you want to pay me the salary I'd need."

"No shit, Sherlock! The in-house part is only gonna be a part of your business, and I'm gonna pay you for the work you done for me. You'd build your practice with other clients with my work bein' the base that gives you like a head start. And I got space for your office; Cohen says whatever the rent is it's gonna be lowered by a credit or somethin' for the amount of your work you done for me. Cohen'll go over the details witcha in a way that you're gonna understand. Whatdya think?"

"Well ... that makes sense. I do have some prospective clients from my days at the firm where I worked before G&A. They are about to grow in new directions and approached me to represent them."

"That's great. Now, you also gonna need somebody to give you a hand. You know, to run the office and handle the details that a high almighty lawyer like you ain't gonna wanna be bothered with."

"I would not put it quite like that, but you are right and I'd want someone with solid paralegal experience, but folks with those skills don't come cheap."

"Well, cousin Francesca got 'em skills. You know, Uncle Tom's and Aunt Helen's younger daughter. She works for one of 'em other fancy, schmancy firms, like your old one, and they work her ass off and she's miserable. So, I says to her is all the money they pay you worth the aggravation you gotta put up with? She says not really, but the dough's so attractive, but on the other hand, she's developin' ulcers, has trouble sleepin' and her husband Jimmy's pissed that she's barely home and when she is, she's like a bitch-on-wheels. And on top of all that she tells me people don't leave that firm on their feet. They're either carried out on a friggin' stretcher or led out in a straitjacket.

"So, she ain't gonna refuse a reasonable offer, with decent pay, decent hours, as long as you ain't drive her outa her friggin' mind. Know what I mean? Jimmy makes a good buck, so this thing they call 'quality of life' could make up for whatever you can't afford to pay her. Whatcha think?"

"Sounds sensible, Mick. I really do appreciate your going out of your way to help me now when I need all the help I can get."

"Al, Al. Come on! We're cousins. We growed up together. I'm, what, eight years older; you're the kid brother I ain't never had. I looked out for you when you was a kid. Then you go off to the high falutin' schools that you went to and we ain't in touch for too long a time. And I'm off doin' my separate thing, and outa commission for a time too, but here we are and blood's thicker than everythin' else and we gotta always watch out for each other. If we ain't gonna watch out for each other who the fuck's gonna do it? *Gabbish?*"

My cousin Mick's father was my father's brother, and Mick followed his dad's footsteps in numbers running and lending money. Uncle Nicola (or Nick) never had the stomach to break legs. Luckily, his wife, my Aunt Tessie, had a brother, Mick's Uncle Louie, who was a sharp lawyer back in the day and suggested to Uncle Nick that he take property as collateral for his loans. This way, if someone defaults, Uncle Nick would foreclose and either get paid off at the auction sale or take the property. After a while Uncle Nick has an inventory of real estate and found himself in the property management business, which Mick would eventually take over and expand.

After giving it considerable thought and discussing it at greater depth with Joe Cohen, and with my wife's necessary blessings, I hang my proverbial shingle at office space leased to me by Mick.

CHAPTER 4

"My last and only hope!"

"AL, A MARY WOODLEY is on line three," Francesca informs me through the intercom.

I pick up the phone and blurt out: "Mary, how've you been? What? It's been two years since we last saw each other? You know I tried to reach you the week after I left, but whoever replaced you said you left and before I could get any information out of her, Gilbert, who must have been standing right there, picked up the phone and told me to blow off. You know, I feel absolutely terrible about what happened to you, and was so frustrated that I was helpless to stop that asshole."

"Don't worry about that. The e-mail you sent Mr. Bellamy, the Executive Committee chair, got Gilbert in some hot water. It has to be the first time the firm had the balls to call Gilbert on the carpet."

"I was so pissed at Gilbert and at myself for being an ineffective wimp that I got up the next morning and wrote a blow-by-blow description of the incident and sent it to Bellamy.

"But, Mary, that's in the past. How've you been? It's really great to hear from you."

"Al, it's not in the past. What happened then still haunts me."

"But Mary, let go of that bully's bullshit. That happened a couple of years ago."

"Listen, I need to meet with you. I need your help. You don't know the full story. I have no money; I'm on welfare with a one-year-old. Can I come by this morning?"

"Gosh! I am late with a memo for an important client .... "

"Al, I'm desperate and every day is critical. I have a case that has to be brought right away."

"Mary, I don't litigate; you know that."

"I've exhausted all other possibilities. There's no one else I can turn to." She is crying now.

"What's been going on? Okay, okay, tell you what, come by at two o'clock. That will give me enough time to finish this bloody thing, but I will have to refer you to another attorney if it involves litigation."

"Al, no one else will touch it. It involves Gilbert. After the firm dissolved, he was appointed a deputy mayor."

"Yeah, I know that. With all the power he wields I'm sure that was a smooth transition. And I'm told he's more of a prick and a bully than ever. But, wait. What's this about Gilbert?"

"I will tell the whole story when I see you. "

"And what happened to Bruce? I see he's been burning up the charts."

"We broke up over this thing with Gilbert. Listen, I can't go over it over the phone. I'll be there at two."

G&A had hired Mary as its night receptionist several years after I started there. She was a graduate student working on a doctorate in philosophy. She was in her mid-twenties at the time and adopted the punk style of hair and dress. She was finishing her coursework and would eventually start researching and writing her dissertation. She was extremely intelligent and whenever we chatted, she amazed me with how sharp she was. We further connected by my getting her former landlord to return her security deposit; he had given her the runaround and I read him the riot act, as it is a misdemeanor not to return a tenant's security deposit. Mary was so appreciative that she had an exquisite arrangement of birds of paradise delivered to my house.

Despite being disturbed by Mary's cryptic story, knowing she'd be here at two forced me to focus and get that damn memo done. I was proofing it and making final edits when she walked in around one.

I recognized her, but barely. Her punk look is gone. She looks more like a hippie from the sixties, dressed in what looked like second-hand clothes, which I soon found out, they were.

"Mary, I almost didn't recognize you. You are so good looking. Your old hairstyle hid the real you."

"Listen Al, I appreciate the compliment, but there is something that I need to get out before I burst.

"Here's the story: Because of Gilbert's stupid temper tantrum on your last day, the Executive Committee demanded that Gilbert apologize to me. Maybe the firm was afraid I would sue for harassment or something. Anyway, they forced Gilbert and Joan Zakorski to take me to dinner to make amends. Gilbert's secretary called to set it up and I would have taken Bruce but he was tied up with a recording session. The firm sent a limo to pick me up and take me to the 21 Club where Gilbert and Zakorski were already drinking.

"I was amazed by how charmingly they treated me, especially Gilbert, who floored me with such a sweet apology. I thought to myself, 'Maybe, I had this guy all wrong. Could he be under such incredible pressure that no one ever witnessed this other side?' I was quite taken aback.

"Anyway, after a couple of drinks at the bar, we moved into the dining area. It is such a lovely restaurant. You ever been there?"

"I haven't and I'll consider going if I ever win the lottery," I say.

"So, we are eating our chateaubriand, a little fancy for me, when Joan gets an urgent call and proceeds to participate in a conference call for some megadeal right at the table, until Gilbert, in an amazingly polite manner, so unlike Gilbert, suggests she take the call elsewhere or go back to the office.

"So, Joan left in the middle of dinner. She called about an hour later to say that she had to stay on top of what was happening with that deal and could not rejoin us. I was alone with Gilbert. We discussed philosophy and music and art. He was breathtaking. And I was feeling a bit overwhelmed by this man I had perceived to be a monster.

"I was so mesmerized by his intellect and, I admit, I had had too much to drink that I agreed to go with him to listen to some music. We got into the limo and drove to a couple of clubs. Gilbert seemed so hip; I was really carried away. We kept downing drinks and we smoked some weed that appeared out of nowhere."

She must have noticed my furrowed brow, but she continued: "Well, Cinderella's slipper soon turned to shit, for the next thing I know I wake up at eight the next morning in some strange, but really fancy, apartment. I don't know how and certainly not why, but I ended up naked in bed with Gilbert in his *pied-à-terre* at The Olympiad.

"I was so mortified. I did not say a word to him, threw on my clothes and ran out as fast as I could.

"Luckily, Bruce was not at our apartment when I got home. He had left a message on the apartment's phone that he had to pull an all-nighter in his studio. I got myself cleaned up fast and left Bruce a note saying I was going to the library to do some research. Instead, I went to my friend Sondra's house and tried to recreate what happened. She tried to be helpful by convincing me that there was nothing to worry about; you know, if he screwed me, he must have used a rubber, and so on. I'm sure he did fuck me because I felt some soreness around my vagina. Anyway, I decided that Sondra was right and I put it out of my mind, until I began to have these cravings for all kinds of weird combinations of food and put on weight for the first time in my life.

"I finally went to the clinic and learned I was four months pregnant. I prayed, like I never prayed before, and I hadn't prayed since Catholic grammar school, that it was Bruce's kid, or at worse, if it wasn't, that Bruce would not doubt that it was his.

"No such luck. Bruce had been really busy and we had hardly had sex and he was so fastidious about birth control. He expressed surprise from the first moment. He said dumb things like no wonder my mother named me Mary, that this was an immaculate conception. Still, he did help me until Roger was born. Then, he insisted on a paternity test and the test showed that there was no way that Bruce was Roger's father. Bruce moved out that night and I haven't heard a word from him since.

"I was devastated. We were together seven years and I had to screw it up this way.

"I never finished my doctorate, which is on hold, and I stopped working after I learned I was pregnant. Now, I am virtually on the street, without savings or a job. I had alienated my parents a long time ago, but I did call them, only to have them slam down the phone on me.

"I was past desperation. I began to call Gilbert and could not get him on the phone. I went to his office and security removed me from the building and told me I'd be arrested for trespassing if I ever returned. I want him to take responsibility for our son, I want the financial support I can't provide."

"Did you see an attorney?"

She blows air out of her nose, which makes her head move back signifying "Did I ever!"

"I went to Legal Aid."

"They should be able to help you, no?"

"They were very interested at first, but they eventually gave me some bullshit about my having assets that I had somehow hidden and did not qualify for their services. At the same time, I read in the papers they are having this budget hassle and who is representing the mayor in those negotiations? None other than Gilbert. I think he got to them in one of his devious ways. So, I'm cut off from free legal assistance. On top of all this, I am at war with social services, for they also became convinced that I have somehow squirreled away assets and don't qualify for assistance, which will be cut off effective the end of next month."

"But you did not consent to the intercourse, so it sounds like you were raped. Did you go to the DA?"

"I did. As soon as I learned that Roger wasn't Bruce's I went there and explained everything to the Sex Crimes Unit."

"What did they do?"

"Asked me all kinds of questions. Once they heard it was Gilbert, it took a whole different tone. In the end, I was told that it was not a clear-cut rape, because it's possible that Gilbert and I were both so drunk at the time that neither of us knew what we were doing. They said they took this up the ladder and a determination higher up was made that no prosecutable crime was committed."

"How are you going to support yourself?"

"That's the big question, isn't it! Because I can't afford child care, it's hard to find work I can do. A nun I met at the Catholic Worker said she can help me line up people to watch Roger so I could take part-time jobs, like waitressing; otherwise, I will do freelance writing and research work, but that is sporadic and doesn't really pay well and what happens when Roger gets sick?

"Anyway, the little I learned is that I am losing money each day that a petition for child support isn't filed. Any retroactive support goes back to that date, so time's critical, unless …."

She pauses and I ask, "Unless what?"

"Well, I was hoping that you would represent me and file the papers ASAP."

"Mary, you know that I certainly would help if I could, but you also know that I am no litigator. My practice is and always has been real estate. And I know just about nothing about family law. I do have a colleague who owes me favors. Peg Wells is an accomplished practitioner in family law, which covers paternity and child support. Let me call her to see if she'll represent you. We'll figure out later how she gets paid."

I dial Peg's number. She's a law school classmate who has called me frequently to pick my brain about real estate practice issues. I bailed her out many a time, and she has acknowledged as much.

"Good afternoon, Margaret Wells's office."

"Hello, Virginia, this is Al Forte. Is Peg available?"

"Oh, hi Mr. Forte. Sorry, but she's on the phone. But, Mr. Forte, did you hear she's been offered the chief clerk's position with Family Court? She's so excited!"

As my heart sinks, Peg picks up and says, "Al, how you've been? I assume your practice is lucrative and you'll soon be able to retire."

"Not a day before I'm seventy-five at the rate I'm going. Anyway, Peg, I have an old friend of mine here with me who has a major problem and I am hoping you will be able to help her."

"Oh, Al, I know I owe you my first born, for all the messes you rescued me from, but the call I was just on was from the chief judge of the Family Court and I accepted his offer to become the chief clerk of that court. I want to be a judge and this will be a means to expedite a judgeship."

"Congratulations. Virginia mentioned that was in the works. But what is your timing? Mary here needs someone to commence a paternity and child support action pronto. Perhaps you can handle it and maneuver a settlement prior to suit."

"Who is the defendant?"

"It happens to be my former boss, Gordon Gilbert."

"Is your former boss the same Gordon Gilbert who was recently made first deputy mayor?"

"One and the same."

"Oh shit! My friend Andrea's father is a major contributor to the mayor and has incredible influence with him and he's became chummy with Deputy Mayor Gilbert. Andrea got her dad to talk to Gilbert, who talked to the chief judge of the Family Court, and that is how I got my appointment. So, I cannot help you. Sorry. And, you know what? No regular practitioner in that Court is likely going to touch it. You need to either get an outsider who will be at a disadvantage because so many of the Court's procedures are quirky and known only to those who appear there regularly."

"You said 'either,' but only gave one option."

"Or *you* learn what has to be done and do it yourself."

"Peggy, how can I? Besides being overworked, I know diddly about litigation in general and less than diddly about paternity/child support suits. Also, I have a history with Gilbert. He hates my guts."

"Al, listen, I am sorry, but I have to get off. It's Gilbert's office on the other line. There's a reception for my predecessor and they want me there. I really want to help any way I can but realistically I can't. I begin in two weeks and it's going to take me no less than four weeks to close out my practice, so I won't even have the time to coach you. So sorry. Let's wish each other luck."

"Yeah, lots of luck." Peg Wells hangs up on "lots."

I notice that Mary's face grows more and more distraught as she listens to my end of the conversation.

She begins to cry, "Al, what am I going to do! You must help me. I have nowhere else to turn, except to you. And if you can't help me, my baby and I are cut off with nothing. You are my last and only hope!"

I had learned that you should always have tissues around in case you encounter a crying client, and my box was just in reach. I could use one myself as well.

CHAPTER 5

"A run for your money."

FRANTIC RESEARCH OF the law and procedure pertaining to paternity and child support suits consumed the better part of the next week. On paper, what had to be done appeared to be straightforward, but Peg's words about how Family Court can be a minefield to the uninitiated were on my mind. Luckily, a few of my major real estate closings were delayed of their own accord and I could steer other matters to more distant dates to free up the time I needed to figure out how to help Mary.

The law is clear: If you parent a child, you are obligated to care for the child, including financially. First, we need a paternity test to prove that Gilbert is the father. Once paternity is established, a determination will be made, based on his income and other financial resources, as to his child support obligation, which would also include his share (relative to Mary's, which would be based on her meager financial status) of the costs for child care, health care, and education. Regarding child support, the law has a formula. For those whose gross income is no more than $143,000, 17 percent of gross income (less some deductions) is the amount due for basic child support.

As Gilbert is a government official, it is a matter of public record that his annual salary is $250,000. For those whose income exceeds $143,000, the court can adjust the 17 percent requirement based on the person's total financial situation. The amount of child support and the share of the other items are subject to annual adjustment based on changes in the cost of living, as well as a change in circumstance, such as job change or bankruptcy.

I figured that Mary would be entitled to child support of around $25,000 per year—based on 17 percent of $143,000—and likely more. On top of that, Gilbert would also have to pay his annual "share" of child care, medical expenses—which includes the premiums for Roger's health insurance policy and all out-of-pocket expenses, like copays and deductibles—and educational costs. Gilbert's share again would be based on his relative wealth compared to Mary's. Then, again, all of this would be subject to annual adjustment.

After giving this considerable thought, I concluded that it would be in Gilbert's best interest to avoid the publicity of a paternity and child support contest by settling out of court pursuant to an agreement that imposed ironclad confidentiality requirements on both sides. This would spare him and the mayor embarrassment. It would also avoid the negative impact on Gilbert's reputation, influence, and future career path, and avoid wreaking havoc on Gilbert's family life.

On Mary's side, she would want to avoid dealing with Gilbert on an annual basis. Even if the obligation to make annual child support payments would be overseen by the court and by the city's social service agency, it would be in Mary's and Roger's best interests to minimize, really eliminate, ongoing contact with Gilbert. Among other things, in his current position, and as a person with great power and influence, Gilbert could unduly influence the social service agency and even the court in future years.

In other words, I concluded that we needed to settle this out of court with all the terms, especially monies due, set in stone and fully paid or otherwise secured, and where confidentiality was the bedrock that held the whole thing together.

Mary and I would further need to confer with a financial expert to help us to project both the maximum and minimum amounts needed to fund Roger's financial needs over the course of his childhood, so we would be appropriately guided in negotiating a settlement.

I fully understood that there is a major risk in negotiating an out-of-court settlement. We risked underestimating Roger's needs. However, I concluded that the far greater risk would be to have to fight with Gilbert every year for the money due, having to be in and out of court with him. And there would be serious complications if Gilbert declared bankruptcy or moved out of state or died.

Of secondary importance, settling this out of court also benefited me, given my limited resources and my unfamiliarity with the system. Additionally, if this went to court, Gilbert would pull out all stops and have an army of attorneys work to drag out the proceedings and wear me down. I assumed this would be offset to a certain extent by the desire on Gilbert's part to avoid embarrassing publicity.

I had phone meetings with Mary and met her in person several times to explain all this to her, and she eventually came to the same conclusion. She agreed that she would want as little as possible to do with Gilbert and that she needed a set amount that was funded or otherwise secured up front, with no possibility of change. She also appreciated that she would likely be accepting less than Roger would be entitled to under the usual route where the annual payments are governed by Family Court and social services, but that route depended on Gilbert doing the right thing every step of the way, which we concurred was unrealistic to expect.

Mary and I also agreed that before we wasted much time spinning our wheels, I needed to test our assumptions and see if Gilbert was willing to negotiate an out-of-court settlement. The problem is that Gilbert hates my guts. This made it very difficult, if not impossible, for me to contact him. Even if I could get him on the phone, he'd likely just hang up on me. I called Keith Young, another former G&A attorney. Keith was politically savvy and he suggested that I use Joan Zakorski as an intermediary. This made sense. Joan was the G&A partner closest to Gilbert and, significantly, she knew that Gilbert and Mary were alone the night in question.

When G&A disbanded, Joan went with several of the partners and some associates to Feiner & Brongberg, another real estate boutique.

When I call her office, Joan's current secretary says Joan is on a conference call and takes my name and number. In response to her query about the subject matter of my call, I inform her it is about Gordon Gilbert. The secretary acknowledges, "Oh yes, the deputy mayor. He calls here often."

I leave messages for Joan for three consecutive days. Her secretary promises each time that she will get Joan to return my call but I know no one could tell Joan what to do. When my calls are not returned by the fourth day, I tell the secretary to inform Joan I am calling about Gilbert and the child he had with Mary Woodley.

Five minutes later, Joan calls.

"Al, what the fuck are you talking about? What's happened to you? Just because you got fired, you have to defame Gordon? Why the fuck are you bothering him? And me?"

I had prepared for Joan's onslaught. With the firmest voice I could muster: "Joan, calm down and listen to me. First, Mary and Gilbert did have a kid together. It happened that night you and Gilbert took her to the 21 Club; you left early to handle some emergency. Second, I apologize for dragging you into this, but you are the only intermediary I know. I don't want to drag this through the press. I want to work it out privately, if possible. It will be in everyone's best interest—Gilbert's, Mary's, and the child's."

Joan is quiet for a few moments. Deep down, she had to know that I would not throw around false statements about anyone.

"Shit! Okay, how do you think I could help?"

"I don't have a means of approaching Gilbert. I need you as someone he trusts to relay my message. Mary just wants child support for their kid. We want to see if Gilbert is willing to enter into negotiations and attempt to settle this matter out of court—and confidentially. But also make clear to Gilbert that we are prepared to take him to court, with all the press around, if he blows us off or jerks us around."

Joan asks the question I knew was coming: "Who has Mary retained to bring the proceeding if Gilbert refuses to negotiate or if she and he can't come to terms?"

"I am ready to do it."

Joan guffaws. "Excuse me for laughing, but you don't know shit about Family Court stuff, let alone any kind of serious litigation."

She is right, but I respond, "Joan, you don't know what kind of matters I have been handling since G&A, so don't rush to judgment."

"You're bluffing, but I really don't care. I'll call Gilbert. But, let me warn you, Gilbert will find out if you have ever set foot in Family Court and, unless he is willing to settle out of court, he will give you a run for your money."

I think to myself: There ain't no money for me to run after.

Joan says, "Give me a few days to get back to you."

"Thanks, Joan."

CHAPTER 6

"What's the worst that can happen?"

"I spoke to Joan, today."

"How did you ever get her on the phone?"

"Persistence, and after three failed attempts, I mentioned I was calling about the child you and Gilbert had together."

"Do you think she knows what happened that night?"

"I don't think so. Nothing she said indicated she did."

"So, what did you say? And what did she say?"

"Basically, I want to use her as an intermediary to get to Gilbert to see if we can settle this thing without having to litigate."

"I know we both agree that a confidential settlement is best, but do you really think he'll be willing to settle?"

"Your guess is as good a mine, but he is a deputy mayor and if such a lawsuit got out, as we discussed, it will certainly be an embarrassment to him and may just ruin any political ambitions he has. Also, it would make the mayor look bad to have someone in his inner circle who fathered a child outside of wedlock and now refuses to accept responsibility for that child.

"Let me break this to you as bluntly as I can: You are laying your hopes at the foot of a non-litigator who, if we must sue, will be up against attorneys who specialize in litigation, who have almost unlimited resources, and who will stop at virtually nothing to squash us. Also, I've always felt that going to court is the same as going to Atlantic City, meaning that the outcome is decided by rolling dice; no matter how good your arguments are, the outcome is impossible to predict."

Mary says, "I know you are committed to get Roger and me child support whether it's in or out of court. Maybe, you should start to believe in yourself."

Francesca then appears at my door, "Al, there's a Joan Something, who thinks she is God's gift to the legal profession, on the phone. She insists that I interrupt."

"Mary, Joan is on the other line. Let me call you back."

"Al, do a conference call so I could hear what she has to say. Don't tell her I'm on."

"Absolutely not, for reasons too numerous to state. I'll call you back; just sit tight."

"Damn you, Al!"

"Calm down and wait for me to call you back."

I hang up on Mary and pick up Joan's call.

"Joan, thanks for getting back to me. Sorry you had to hold."

"Listen, if you want me to be in the middle of this thing, I don't want to wait for you to take my calls."

I ignore what she said and ask, "Did you speak with Gilbert?"

"Yes, and his attorney too. You know John Stillman of Adler & Stillman?"

"I never met him, but I know of him of course." And of his reputation as being one of the toughest, and meanest, litigators in town.

"Well, they want to sit down with you tomorrow at my office at 8 a.m."

"Joan, this is short notice and so early." I could feel my bowels move.

"These are extremely busy people. You're lucky they are making any time for you."

I hesitate, thousands of thoughts and doubts troubling me.

"Al, you still there? I need to get back to them."

"Alright, alright, I'll be there, but I don't know if Mary could make it."

"If she shows up, they will walk out. They want to meet with you alone."

"I think she should be there in case they make an offer. It could expedite a settlement."

"They insist attorneys only. They probably want to make an offer that'd be better for you to review with her alone, so she won't feel pressured to decide on the spot. They want to wrap this up posthaste. Besides, they want to avoid a scene with your client getting all emotional, yelling and carrying on."

A thought comes to me. "Joan, am I being set up for some kind of ambush?"

"Al, you have stuck me in the middle of something I truly want nothing to do with. You requested that I make contact. I did that. All I know is that they are willing to meet and get this behind them. They revealed nothing else to me. And this is starting to take up more of my time than I have to give you."

"Okay, okay. Thanks. I think I can trust you."

"That's not the issue. I do not care whether you think I am trustworthy. I don't need your approval, so please don't patronize me and just show up on time tomorrow."

Joan hangs up. Before I could consider what just happened, Francesca is at the door to announce that Mary had called back right away and insisted to be put on hold and then connected to me the second I finished with Joan.

"So, what's the story? Are we going to court?"

"For the moment, no. Gilbert and his attorney want to meet with me alone tomorrow."

"Al, I want to be there too. I also want to bring Roger, so that prick can be confronted by the son he wants to have nothing to do with."

"Joan said they will walk out if you show up. They said they want to avoid a scene."

"Well fuck them! They don't want a scene? That prick Gilbert should have thought of that before he screwed me. That bastard! "

"Listen, Joan also said they want to present their proposal to me and then have me take it to you so we can discuss it fully without pressuring you to make a decision on the spot."

"That's bullshit. I smell a rat. I think they are setting a trap for us, really."

"I'm aware of that possibility and asked Joan whether I will be ambushed?"

"And?"

"And she got annoyed, but did assure me that there will be an offer."

"I doubt it."

"Listen, I will go and see what happens. What's the worst that can happen? They make a bullshit offer and we spit in their faces—literally, of course."

"I would love to spit in Gilbert's face before this is over."

"Look, it's getting late. I need to make some calls for tomorrow's meeting. I wish I had more time to prepare."

"By the way, who's representing Gilbert? Joan?"

"No, she's only the intermediary. It's this hotshot John Stillman of Adler & Stillman."

"Isn't that that firm with a terrible reputation."

"It's a firm with all of the right connections and one that rarely loses. High-powered, very aggressive, and very tough, rough would be more accurate. Like Gilbert, cutthroat even."

"If it doesn't work out tomorrow, we will be facing that firm in court?"

"I guess so."

"Oh, shit. This is what you have been talking about."

"You got it. But listen, don't let that worry you just yet. Really, we'll fight the hardest we can for little Roger."

"You don't know how reassuring that is to me. I was worried that you might wimp out on us, the way you were talking earlier. I was scared you were having a crisis of confidence, but I said to myself that that couldn't be possible. I understand you're only trying to help me understand how tough the fight will be, right?"

"Sure, without a doubt. Now let me go so I'll be ready for tomorrow."

There are two calls I must make. The first, to Peg Wells to beg for guidance with the negotiations; the other to my cousin, Mick Forte, to help me navigate my way to the meeting on time. As Mick is the more elusive of the two, I beep him first and figure I'd have enough time to pick Peg's brains before Mick responds.

Peg's office phone has a message that her number is no longer in service. I figure she closed her shop and is either already in her new Family Court position or taking some time off before assuming that post. I call her at home.

"Peg, I'm glad I caught you."

"You're lucky to catch me at all; you got me as I am walking out the door. Car service will be here to take me to the airport any minute now. I have an out-of-town funeral."

"My condolences."

"Thanks. It's for a distant family member. What's up?"

"Remember that case I mentioned to you a few weeks ago, involving Deputy Mayor Gilbert?"

"Ah, yeah, yeah. I do vaguely. A lot's been happening with this new job and closing the office, my mind is pre-occupied—I'm a bit overwhelmed. But I do recall that I can't take on the case due to my new position and that I won't be able to get too involved even informally because of Gilbert's position and Family Court politics."

"I wish my 'vague recollections' were so vivid. But, I just need to pick your brains for a minute on black letter stuff, because I have a meeting that may become a negotiating session with Gilbert and his attorneys in the morning and I need your gut feeling as to what a reasonable settlement would be, assuming we can settle and not need to resort to litigation."

"Gee, it's impossible for me to give you any meaningful guidance. It all depends on Gilbert's income, assets, and other obligations ... Wait, that's my cab. Listen, I don't mean to cut you off, but I must go, otherwise I'll miss my plane. I'll call you at home tonight. You'll be in around ten this evening?"

"Absolutely. I will get screwed without guidance from someone with your kind of experience. Thanks."

We both hang up. Shit! I think to myself, this does not bode well.

Just then, Francesca announces that Mick is on the other line.

"Mick, I need to get to midtown tomorrow morning by eight. I don't trust the subway to get me there on time at that hour and I can't be late for this meeting."

"Only rat bastards ain't got nuttin' better to do than get people up and runnin' around at that time of day. Okay, let me think. Oh yeah, I gotta take this lady to Grand Central for a 7:30 train tomorrow morning. Works perfect. You hitch a ride with us."

"Mick, you sure you'll have enough room? She's not going to have a lot of luggage, is she?"

"Nah, should be good. I come by at 6:30. You be down, okay?"

"Great. Thanks, Mick, I knew I could count on you."

"You can't count on me, then life ain't worth livin', my friend. See you in the mornin'. Just gotta warn you the lady is a real bitch and a half, so there's gonna be some yellin' back and forth between us. So, it ain't gonna be the most pleasant of rides."

"No problem. See you in the morning, Mick. Thanks."

One of the legitimate businesses Mick has is a car service. He started it to keep his maintenance crew busy and as a sideline to his property management business, as he would offer his senior tenants rides to the grocery and the doctor when his crew wasn't busy. It assists in tenant relations.

After dinner, I sit at my home desk gathering my thoughts for tomorrow's meeting. A bit after nine, the phone rings.

"Peg, great! Thanks for calling and even early."

"Al, I can't talk long. I got a call just as I boarded the plane. They know—don't ask me how—that you have been in touch with me and I have been warned that if I even speak to you, that I will lose the chief clerk job. I'm calling you with a disposable phone, because I felt I at least owed you the courtesy of a call to let you know this. Bye, and good luck."

She hangs up. I couldn't get a word in. I'm flabbergasted, ready to erupt. I wish I could have asked Peggy if that job was more important than the firstborn she claimed I was owed. Now, I'm really stuck, with little clue as to what the settlement terms should be. I have no choice but to wing it and pray for the best. This is frightening enough without considering who the "they" were she mentioned, and how anyone could know we were talking. It's unsettling to say the least.

I had asked Mary, "What's the worst that can happen?" I now feared the answer to that previously rhetorical question.

CHAPTER 7

"Thanks for the pep talk."

MICK IS DOWNSTAIRS the following morning at 6:15 sharp. I knew he would be early so I'm ready early and keep looking out the window for him.

Soon as I open the car door, I could hear what Mick had warned me about.

"Lady, you wanna stop bitchin'? I told you I hafta drop my cousin off near Grand Central. You ain't gonna miss your friggin' train. I guarantee you that you'll either catch your train or I'll personally deliver you to White Plains before the time your train's supposed to get there. So, please shut up already; you're aggravatin' me."

I say, "I'm sorry, ma'am, if I'm causing any trouble."

"Al, no, you ain't. Say hello to Miss Worry here, settle your ass in the car and let's get the fuck on our way to the station."

"Mick, please, you have a lady here."

"Al, stop with the altar boy bullshit. This is the way it is. Ain't no use dressin' it up. Besides, all my customers know how I am and if they don't like it, they can take their lives in their hands and use one of 'em other car services or the subway and get late to where they gotta go."

Since I got into Mick's car, we had traveled only one block. Normally, there is no parking allowed on Smith

Street until after 10 a.m. to accommodate the morning rush. This morning there are emergency vehicles doubled-parked on the next block, forcing three lanes to merge into one, limiting traffic to a crawl.

Mick opens his window and shouts to the driver of the nearest emergency vehicle, "God damn it, Jimmy Tomato, why the fuck are youse sittin' on your fat asses blockin' rush hour traffic and I ain't even seein' no emergency?"

"O Christ, if it ain't Mick the Quick. To tell the truth, Quickie, none of us knows what we're doin' here with our thumbs up our butts. They only dispatch us when there's an emergency. Today, they tell us to go over to Smith and Pacific and wait for further orders. God forbid, there's some trouble the other side of Brooklyn.

"Tell you what, Mick, I'll get the fuckers ahead of me to move and go around the block and come back. You get behind me and follow me so you can get outa my face. How's that, you no good bastard?"

"Thanks a lot, asshole, just don't let this happen again."

"Mick, you really know everyone, don't you?" I ask.

"Yep, I got good connections. Jimmy's brother and I were in the joint together. If it ain't for me, Lenny never wudda made it."

From that point on traffic is heavy but moving slowly, but Mick, in his own inimitable fashion, manages to maneuver to Grand Central with more than ample time for his passenger to make her train. Upon arrival, Mick parks illegally in front and tells me, "I'm walkin' Miss Worry here to her train. Any traffic cop comes, let 'em know I'll be right back."

"But Mick leave me your keys so I can move the car to avoid your getting ticketed or towed. I'll go around the block and should be back by time you return."

"No, absolutely ain't necessary. Just say Mick Forte'll be right back."

I continue to protest but Mick waves me off and hustles into the terminal with his passenger.

The precise moment Mick disappears through the terminal's door, out of the rear-view mirror I see a traffic enforcement tow truck approach and pull in front of Mick's car. Then, I spot a traffic enforcement officer on foot approach Mick's car from the front. I'm panicked and afraid that this is going to make me late for my meeting and screw everything up for Mary even before I get started.

Both the tow driver and the on-foot officer converge on Mick's car at the same time. The windows being automatic and the ignition off, I had to open the door to talk to them and am stuttering "Hamina, hamina, hamina" in my best Ralph Kramden imitation, when the tow driver says, "Hey, be sure to tell Mick that Bobby Jo the tow driver and my supervisor Sully here are sorry we missed him and send our best. Tell him, too, that my mother-in-law who's one of his tenants appreciates how quick his super replaced her washing machine. My wife tells me that her mother discovered it was broke yesterday at nine in the morning and by two a brand-new one was delivered, installed, and up and running. She's so grateful." With that, they go off and Sully tickets the car that is parked behind Mick's and Bobby Jo maneuvers his truck so he could tow it.

Mick is back about five minutes later. I tell him about Bobby Jo's and Sully's visit. He says, "Sorry I missed 'em. A coupla real nice guys." And off we go. But for my being all stressed out about the upcoming meeting, I would have tried to get to the bottom of what just transpired, but I just let it go.

"That passenger sure is a first-class ballbuster. All the time she drives me outa my friggin' mind. You know how some dames just rub you the wrong way? They get unda your skin and you just wanna belt 'em one. It's bad enough when it's your old lady, you're married to her, that's part of the 'for worse' that goes with the 'for better,' but when it's just some customer, you just wanna tell her to just shut the fuck up or remove her voice box withcha bare hands."

"Calm down, Mick. That's the price of having to deal with the public; you get all kinds."

"Ain't that the God-honest truth."

I told Mick nothing about the meeting I was attending. He offers to wait to take me back to my office, but I tell him to get his ass back to Brooklyn and make some money, so that one day the only living he makes is a legal one.

He responds, "That'll be the day. At least you ain't say an honest livin'."

"Mick, if you're anything, you're honest. Everyone who knows you knows that.

"Here's the building. Thanks a lot for the lift."

"Call me later and let me know how this meetin' went. I got a funny feelin' about it, even though you ain't tell me shit about it. Don't let 'em jerk you off. Show 'em you are tough, couldn't give a fuckin' shit about their threats, and you ain't gonna back down no matter what."

"Mick, you're clairvoyant."

"Hey, *va fa gool a sodida*! Why the fuck you insult my manhood and call me a women's name? I'm only tryin' to give you the best advice I got."

"Mick, you idiot, clairvoyant isn't a women's name. It means you can read people's minds. You must have been sick the day it was covered in the seventh grade."

"You know, the seventh grade was the two happiest years of my yout."

"Anyway, I do appreciate the pep talk. I need the boost. This is gonna be a real tough one."

"Al, all I wantcha to know is that of all us cousins, you the only one who did all this school stuff. Ain't nobody in our families who's a lawyer, other than my mom's brother, but he was one in the old days. We got plenty of garbage mens, construction workers, taxi drivers; you know, basically workin' stiffs who hardly made enough to get by til 'em unions got some power. But we ain't got nobody who's like a real professional, who went as far as you. Maybe, we ain't said nuttin' to you, but we admire you, 'cause like me, it ain't hard for me to start doin' the numbers and loan business, 'cause my dad did 'em, so I seen what they were about and he showed me what to do. Nobody in the family cudda've done that for you; you hadda do it all by your lonesome.

"So, 'em guys, and ladies too now, who had daddies who were lawyers already knows what it's all about from the inside. So, they, like, have a head start over you. But, you gotta know that the family believes in you and you make us real proud. So, besides doin' good for the client you're workin' for, you do good for us. So, now you go in there and show 'em *stroonzes* you're meetin' with that our people can do what they can, and even better. The mean streets we come from got us ready for all the shit that life brings."

With Mick's encouraging words ringing in my ears, I jump out of the car and head into what I know is the lion's den.

CHAPTER 8

"You should be so lucky."

THE RECEPTIONIST OF Feiner & Brongberg is already on duty. As I approach, she says, "You must be Mr. Forte. You are expected in the main conference room. No one is available to escort you there, but please walk down that corridor. The door is open and you will recognize some of the people there."

There are six people sitting around this huge table, which could probably seat twenty-four comfortably. There are Joan, Gordon Gilbert, and John Stillman, and two whom I presumed from their dress to be associates of either Joan's or Stillman's. The last person is a fortyish African-American fellow who is not in attorney garb, but in a plaid shirt and khakis.

"Since this is my office," begins Joan, "allow me to make the introductions, after which I will leave you all alone to conduct your business. This is Al Forte, who represents Mary Woodley. Al, you know your former colleague, Deputy Mayor Gordon Gilbert. And you must know of John Stillman here of Adler & Stillman. Ethan Jeffers and Elaine Kuby are associates at Adler, and Bill over there is connected with Adler."

Nods and faint smiles are exchanged, except Gilbert looks ahead and lets out sort of a snort. Joan gets up and leaves.

I want to get in the first words, so I take the floor: "As Joan mentioned, I am here as Mary Woodley's attorney. It is my and my client's hope that this matter can be settled expeditiously and amicably out of court."

As I am finishing my remarks, Gilbert lurches forward, only to have Stillman grab his arm and say something in his ear. Whatever he said, Stillman got Gilbert to sit back.

Stillman then leans forward, places his elbows on the table, looks me straight in the eye and says: "My client, the esteemed deputy mayor, and one of the finest attorneys on the planet, does not take kindly to the falsities being spoken about him. It has been brought to our attention that you and your client are spreading false rumors that the deputy mayor impregnated your client and fathered her child."

I immediately interject, "Excuse me. I resent the implication that I am a rumormonger. I did talk to Joan about my client's allegations and neither I nor my client have engaged in any kind of publicity about her claims that in any way, shape, or form can be categorized or construed as the spreading of rumors."

"Excuse me, young man, but we gave you the opportunity to make your remarks without interruption and I would appreciate if you would permit me to also speak without any interference until I am finished. Otherwise, I fear we will go around and around and get nowhere."

Mick would say that he's jerking me off.

"Look, Mr. Stillman, I will not be intimidated by you, the deputy mayor, or anyone else. My client will be taken seriously and I will not allow you to play games with us.

If you have an offer, let me hear it. After all, you people asked for this meeting, and on such short notice."

Stillman clears his throat and proceeds: "As you wish. We deny your client's allegations. Who knows how many sexual partners she has had? She was with that rap artist Bruce; she must be promiscuous. And, Mr. Forte, you are obviously attempting to extract revenge against Mr. Gilbert for his former firm's firing you. As to your client's motivation, it is a money grab on her part, trying to turn an alleged one-night stand into her meal ticket. This attempt to blemish Mr. Gilbert's stellar reputation and to extort money from him will be most vigorously defended and countered."

I stand up, look Stillman in the eye and say, "Let's be clear. You know nothing whatsoever about Mary and her sexual partners. Do not cloud the very simple issue here, for even if the entire Marine Corps had its way with her, our only issue is whether Gordon Gilbert is Roger's father. If he is, then under the law he is obligated to take care of his son financially and otherwise.

"I propose that your client submit to a confidential paternity test. If it establishes that he is Roger's father, as my client and I know it will, then let us proceed to hammer out a strictly confidential out-of-court settlement. Otherwise, we will fight this in court, and your client will have to face whatever publicity comes from that.

"Make no mistake: I will do everything in my power to prevent Gilbert from shirking his responsibility to Mary and Roger. He must 'man up,' like he used to preach to his associates."

With that, Stillman nods to casually-dressed Bill, who approaches me with some papers. When he reaches me, he asks "Al Forte?" I nod and he hands the papers to me and says, "These are for you." And then he leaves the room.

The papers are legal papers. The top page is a summons with the caption naming Gilbert as plaintiff and Mary and myself as defendants. I look up at Stillman and ask, "What is this?"

"As I said, we will not permit the deputy mayor's reputation to be sullied by outrageous claims of some confused and desperate young lady, and her attorney.

"Now, before you get the impression that we look forward to a prolonged and expensive legal battle, let me present our offer.

"First, note that the papers in your hands have no index number for they have not yet been filed with the court; at this juncture, they are mere courtesy copies. Bill, a process server with my office, knows who you are and will serve you and your client personally if we must commence the defamation action those papers represent.

"Nevertheless, we are willing to enter a formal written agreement not to bring that defamation action, provided your client releases the deputy mayor in writing from any paternity and child support claims she thinks she has—and the agreement will expressly state that we deny those claims—in consideration of a one-time payment of $25,000. I hold here an official bank check for $25,000 payable to the order of your client. Our respective clients sign a confidentiality agreement, exchange mutual releases, and the check is in your client's hands.

"Let's be frank with one another. By your coming here this morning to discuss settlement, you recognize what you and your client would be up against if we litigated her outrageous and defamatory claims. Even if you did not have to contend with our defamation action, which I am prepared to commence today, you do not have the resources to go up against us in Family Court. I doubt you have ever set foot in that court. Not that my office is in there regularly, but when we have been, we have tapped resources with extensive experience in that court and with this type of proceeding. Thus, you and your client will be at a terrible disadvantage.

"In that light, our offer of $25,000 is quite generous, but we need to know by the end of business today if your client accepts it."

I stand up and announce, "Lady and gentlemen, this meeting is over. Your offer is rejected and we will see you in court. All I need to do is prove paternity and your client will have no choice but to submit to a paternity test by court order if he refuses to be tested voluntarily. Once paternity is established, I have the basis for the child support claim and an absolute defense to your frivolous defamation action."

Then I think I hear Stillman's associate Ethan Jeffers say, "If you should be so lucky," under his breath.

"Sorry, what did you say?" I ask Jeffers.

"Nothing. Ah, ah, nothing at all," the now red-faced Jeffers responds.

I get up, say, "Bring it on, friends," and walk out of there as fast as I can.

CHAPTER 9

"Up yours!"

"**Welcome back, counselor.** I know you gotta be in the middle of somethin' big, so after I drop you off, I come to see what I could drag outa Francesca. She's tight-lipped, but Mary here come by, and she told me the whole story. When the fuck you gonna let me know about this? You're dealin' with fire and need me to watch your back."

"Mick, please go so I can confer with my client."

Mary says, "Al, Mick can stay. As he said, I filled him in on everything and I trust him."

"So, Mary, you authorize me to inform you about what transpired at the meeting with Gilbert and his attorneys in Mick's presence?"

"Yes," Mary responds.

I explained that they offered to settle with a one-time payment of only $25,000 on a take-it-or-leave-it basis, which I rejected without feeling the need to confer with her about this insult of an offer.

Mary says, "Good. You did the right thing."

"I knew you would concur. And they also said that if we rejected the $25,000, they would bring a defamation action against me and you, Mary, alleging that we're spreading falsehoods about Gilbert's fathering Roger. I am not concerned about any defamation action, as truth is an absolute defense, and once we establish that Gilbert is Roger's father through a paternity test, not only will any defamation suit be dismissed, but Gilbert's obligation to financially support Roger will be established.

"But they absolutely deny any responsibility. I even offered to have the paternity test done confidentially first, and when paternity is established, then proceed to negotiate a strictly confidential out-of-court settlement, but they wouldn't hear of it."

"Okay, so, where we gonna go from here?" Mick asks.

"I serve the papers in Mary's child support action, which will also seek an order requiring Gilbert to submit to a paternity test, and defend the defamation action if it is ever brought," I reply.

Mick shoots back with, "Yeah, come on, what else?"

My rapid response is, "There is nothing else now."

"Oh, yeah," Mick continues, "and whatcha gonna do to protect against the dirty tricks you know they gonna use? Ain't no doubt about it. No bookie gonna take any action that it ain't gonna happen. No way, no how, I'm tellin' you."

"Mick, we don't know that," is my response.

"If you think that, you're settin' yourself and Mary up for somethin' terrible." Mick retorts.

"Mick, I want to be as clear and emphatic as I can be. I am dealing with litigation and that is the only front there is. There is no role whatever for you."

"Pardon me, Mary, but up yours, Al!" Mick responds. He is clearly agitated.

He continues, his face reddening as he growls: "You're kiddin' yourself that this ain't nuttin' except for a simple legal thing. You know that so-and-so Gilbert—Mary, I'm gonna hold my tongue as best I could so you ain't offended—that so-and-so will stop at nuttin' to defeat anyone who dares to go up against him. This ain't no simple legal thing. It's war and there ain't nuttin' that's gonna stop him and his goons from doin' whatever they gotta do to make you and Mary go away. Doncha remember whatcha told me about what he done to clients of the old firm who followed attorneys who left the firm?"

"Yes, of course. While clients are free to change attorneys at will, Gilbert was known to do everything in his power to either bring those clients back or to ruin them in some way. If any of them needed some tax exemption, or a zoning variance, or were sued, Gilbert would somehow pull some strings and reap some sort of retribution.

"That was when G&A was still in business. I do not see how what happened to former G&A clients has anything to do with Mary," I say.

"Well, let me let you know what's it gotta do with Mary," Mick responds. "Why's he hadda go after 'em clients? Ain't you attorneys always gonna replace old clients with new ones? He went after those clients outta spite, s-p-i-t-e, that's spit with an e. He felt dissed and he don't like it when clients leave him. But with Mary, you're goin' after *him*, after *his* money and by doin' whatcha plan to do, you put *his* reputation at stake and screw up *his* career, *his* future. The stakes are a lot bigger here. He's gonna come at youse even stronger. He's gonna do whatever he gotta do to stop you from takin' money from him and from messin' with him in any way. And now doncha forget about his spiteful side, 'cause by time this is over he'll squish you and Mary like grapes.

"You even offered to play nice. You say to him go ahead and get tested in private. And what did he do with your offer? He tells you to shove it up your ass! The way he's gonna play it, he's gonna come out clean and got no worries at all about his money, his reputation, or his career, 'cause you ain't even gettin' to first base!

"So, Mr. Know-It-All, whatcha gonna do when mysterious things start happenin' to you and it's too late to do somethin' about 'em? You need me and my crew to scout out the dirty tricks they plan and cut 'em off at the pass."

"Mick, that is all speculation. You have not an ounce of hard evidence. I cannot act on mere speculation."

Mick says, "Look, there ain't no question that you can handle the legal end; just let me handle the street stuff. Don't forget I got great contacts: law clerks, cops, you name it. I can get information and pull strings like you ain't believe."

I close my eyes and plead, "Please, Mick, I cannot let you run wild and risk running afoul of the rules of legal ethics. It would weaken, or even damage, our position in court. Remember how I was threatened with getting disbarred and you almost arrested for trying to intercede with the city surveyor for my client who needed his condo floor plans reviewed quickly?"

"Please, please, God have mercy on our souls, as I pray for the patience of a saint," Mick is livid now. "I can't for the life of me understand why you don't wanna remember what really happened there. One more time I remind you and let Mary know what it is you bullshittin' about: Sure, they claimed I was tryin' to bribe the city surveyor, and they did say if I did then you might lose your license, 'cause this was all to get special treatment for your client. But there ain't no bribe. I just called in a favor. I did this guy a major solid and expected that if I—or one of my friends, *or relatives*—ever needed a hand that this guy'd help. Now, my old friend Tommy asked me to help the son of this guy, who I don't know at the time is the city surveyor. The kid owed these leg-breakin' loan sharks lots of dough and mouthed off to 'em. It was pure luck that I was the banker for part of these wise guys' business and got 'em to sell me the kid's loan. I then made the terms more manageable. Not only that, I got the kid into drug rehab, run by my pal Alphonse Alba, and the kid's now clean, got a job, paid me off. His dad's happier that a pig rollin' in mud; so, when I call on him to do the right thing for Al's client, the Department of Investigation thinks I'm bribin' the guy and, like you say, threaten me with arrest and you Al with disbarment. Lucky, Tommy's cousin works for the Department of Investigation and tells the investigator on the case the story about the loan sharks, and they realize there ain't no bribe if there ain't no do-re-mi at play. So, that's no big deal and the city surveyor did the right thing by workin' his tail off (for a change) and reviewed all the plans ahead of Al's client and got to that client's plans quick. So, Al, stop with the bullshit that this good deed I done for you was a bad thing, 'cause it ain't. And it hurts me a lot when you say I'd do anythin' that'd screw you in any way."

"Sorry, Mick, but that doesn't change a thing," I said. "The city surveyor situation was resolved the way it was because of pure luck. You happened to know Mr. A who knew Mr. B who knew 'the Man.' Without this lucky coincidence, I still have every confidence it would have been resolved in our favor, but who knows how much time and anxiety it would have taken. And as it was, I did lose plenty of sleep over it.

"This is the bottom line for Mary's matter: I must have total control over this case and under no circumstances can you get in the middle of it without my prior authorization."

"You're such a dope," Mick says with a sigh. "We ain't gonna get no announcement of what Gilbert and his goons are up to. If you ain't got the trust that I'll do everythin' possible to help you to help Mary, all I can say to you, after I apologize to Mary ahead a time for what I'm gonna say, is fuck you very much, and in the end you will find that you got yourself fucked without gettin' laid!"

With that, Mick storms out of the office. Mary has a stunned look on her face.

CHAPTER 10

"You think he would stoop that low?"

"You need to know what you're up against."

"I am fully aware of how hard-charging and cutthroat Adler & Stillman is."

"If that's all you know, you are going into this thing for Mary blind and totally unprepared."

I am sitting in a Starbucks in Glen Ridge, New Jersey, meeting here at the insistence of Molly Howard, a former colleague at G&A, who after its dissolution went with Joan to Feiner & Brongberg.

The morning after the meeting with Gilbert and Stillman at Joan's office, a package with no return address arrives at my office. Inside is one of those disposable cell phones and a note from Molly, asking that I call her that night at nine sharp at a specified phone number.

Puzzled, but trusting Molly, I call her, as requested, using that phone.

"Al, I am so happy you called."

"I am glad to hear from you, Molly. We haven't been in touch much since I left G&A. I'm puzzled by all this cloak-and-dagger stuff though. What's up?"

"You need to know what you're up against by going after Gilbert."

"Oh, I have more than a clue. But how do you know about me and Gilbert?"

"You know I'm working with Joan, and when I saw you were there yesterday, I asked Joan's secretary and she filled me in. I feel so terrible for Mary.

"But, no, you don't have a clue as to what you are up against. We need to have a long conversation. This is what I want you to do. This Saturday, you need to sneak over to New Jersey. Leave your house and drive yourself somewhere to a parking garage where you can leave your car and meet someone else with a car inside the garage who will then sneak you out of that garage unseen—lower yourself in the back seat, if you have to—and take you to Penn Station. At Penn Station, take a New Jersey Transit train that is scheduled to arrive in Glen Ridge around noon; it takes less than an hour to get to Glen Ridge. When you get there, walk to Bloomfield Boulevard, which is a short distance from the train station. You can't miss it. Make a right on Bloomfield and walk several blocks to a Starbucks, where I will be waiting for you."

That Saturday, I drive my car to my parent's assisted living residence, park in its underground garage, and am picked up there by Sammy, one of Mick's car service drivers. Saturday is Sammy's off day, but he agrees to do me this favor, and, more importantly, promises not to mention anything to Mick.

I arrive at the Starbucks in Glen Ridge shortly before noon. Molly is waiting for me.

"Al, it's great to see you, though I wish the circum-stances were different."

"Molly, yes, it's great to see you too, but why this shroud of secrecy?"

Molly had come over to G&A when it merged with her former firm. She's a specialist in intellectual property law, a specialty that G&A lacked.

"Al, you were just about the only decent person at G&A. When I got there, you were the one person who made me feel welcome. Most of the others were alright, but not that personable. And when you left, what little morale the place had just evaporated. When the firm dissolved, I think most of us released a collective sigh of relief.

"Anyway, after the dissolution, Joan asked that I join her in her new firm."

"Yeah, I knew that, but it totally slipped my mind since I was not expecting the meeting to be at your firm's offices. And in any event, we met so early, I never would have expected to see you."

"Actually, I got there right before your meeting ended."

"You should have come over to say hi."

"I would have, but the end of your meeting was so contentious and you stormed out of there in such a rush, I decided to lay low. I figured I would give you a call, but then I overheard something that made me realize that I needed to meet with you secretly."

"What are you talking about, Molly?"

"Well, after you left, both Stillman and Gilbert were screaming at that male associate. He had apparently blurted out something inappropriate. He kept pleading that it was an impulsive remark made under his breath that you seemed to indicate you hadn't heard."

"Yeah, I thought Ethan Jeffers said something but he denied saying anything."

"Well, it was a remark made in response to something you said. He said something like, 'If you should be so lucky.' Gilbert and Stillman took turns reaming him for giving you what they claim was a warning about their strategy."

"That's bizarre. Don't know what that could be referring to. I had just made the point that once we establish paternity, it's full sails ahead for Mary's claim for child support and an absolute defense to any defamation suit they may bring. Which they did bring, by the way."

"Those bastards!"

Soon after Mick stormed out of my office the day of my meeting with Gilbert and pals, Francesca stuck her head into the conference room to say there was someone waiting with an important delivery. It turned out to be Bill, Adler & Stillman's process server. Francesca led him into the conference room, and he proceeded to personally serve both me and Mary with the papers for the defamation suit which Stillman had previously threatened us with. Accompanying the papers was an Order to Show Cause ordering that Mary and I show cause at a hearing, set two weeks hence, why the defamation case shouldn't be sealed and conducted on a strictly confidential basis with the name of the plaintiff remaining anonymous. The papers also imposed temporary restraining orders ordering that pending the hearing on the Order to Show Cause (i) all matters pertaining to the defamation suit be kept strictly confidential; (ii) any publicity of Mary's paternity and child support claims is prohibited; and (iii) no suit can be commenced by Mary regarding those claims. I explained all this to Molly. I also informed her that, but for this prohibition, I would have brought the paternity and child support proceeding in Family Court against Gilbert the following week.

Molly continues, "I've been racking my brain, what strategy could Gilbert and Stillman be alluding to? Well, as you said, you prove paternity, then you're home free. That 'if you should be so lucky' remark by Jeffers rang a bell. There was a very strange thing that happened to this attorney Robert Herman not long after you left the firm."

"I don't think I ever heard of Robert Herman. What's the story?"

"Well, just before my firm merged into G&A, which gave it the capacity to handle intellectual property matters, one of G&A's clients received a letter from Herman on behalf of one of Herman's clients claiming that the G&A client was infringing Herman's client's patent. I heard that Gilbert conferred with G&A's litigation partner who said he'd need to research patent law to give an opinion. Gilbert, who disliked the client, but liked its business, decided not to wait to hear back from the litigation partner and gave off-the-cuff guidance to the G&A client that it was not infringing and even if it were, it was unlikely that Herman's client would bring a suit.

"That was such dumb advice. A cursory look at patent law would have informed Gilbert that a party that proves infringement is entitled to legal fees and that an infringer is subject to treble damages if a valid warning is disregarded. It turns out that was exactly the case there.

"Well, Herman commences a suit on behalf of his client. By this time, my firm is part of G&A and when the case is given to us to handle we give Gilbert the bad news that we have a worst-case scenario to deal with. He flips, of course. Even worse, the G&A client is informed by an attorney relative that Gilbert had given slipshod advice and that the G&A client had a strong malpractice claim against G&A.

"The patent group at G&A advised the client to cease the infringement immediately and that we will try to negotiate the amount of damages in order to limit them. Gilbert agrees and makes a deal with the client that G&A would cover any damages above regular damages. We told Gilbert that we had better put our malpractice insurer on notice, but he refused. He didn't want this to increase our premium and he claimed that even a notice of a claim would result in an increase whether the claim proved to be valid or not. He said that we will, instead, 'vigorously' challenge the claims for legal fees and treble damages. We advised him that that was a long shot. He told us, 'You do your thing, I'll do mine.' Since we were handling the case, we pressed him to let us know what he meant, but he simply smirked and said, 'You shall see.'

"Well, we were frankly shocked with the ultimate outcome, because when it was all done, the G&A client got off scot-free."

"How did you swing that?"

"That's a good question. Here's what happened: There were many adjournments of the date by which we were to submit papers and have oral argument regarding legal fees and damages. Gilbert ordered that we request the adjournments, except for the last one which was necessitated by Herman's getting to court late. He got stuck in some awful traffic jam. So, the judge set a drop-dead date without the possibility of further adjournment.

"On that drop-dead date, the court officers who policed entry into the courthouse were told to wand every attorney, instead of simply allowing attorneys with court-issued passes to walk right through, as per normal procedure. A metal container found in Herman's coat pocket made the wand vibrant. The officer found a plastic bag in the container containing a white powdery substance.

"Herman was beside himself. Because he was a respected attorney, they summoned the officer in charge. An undercover cop from the Narcotics Unit was in some waiting room waiting to be called to testify in some drug case and was asked to give a preliminary opinion about the contents of the container. He reported that it appeared to be cocaine. This left the court officers no choice but to take Herman into custody and to let the system run its course.

"The judge allowed Herman's opposition papers to be taken from his brief case and submitted in lieu of oral argument. None of the other attorneys in Herman's small firm were familiar enough with the case to argue in his place."

"And what happened with the case?"

"Herman's client unexpectedly lost. And Herman had to do time for possession, and was then disbarred. He was subsequently released upon appeal due to the prosecutor's failure to prove intent to either sell or use (because tests of

Herman's blood did not reveal any drug use). His attorney's license was also reinstated. Herman, however, was never the same after that and his stature as an attorney declined significantly. He had several nervous breakdowns and eventually left the practice. So unfortunate."

"Okay, and the point of all this?"

"I must admit that I could not prove it, but I believe that what happened to Herman was somehow orchestrated by Gilbert. And when the associate said the other day 'If you should be so lucky,' he may be referring to something being planned that will undermine your efforts and likely prevent you from ever getting Gilbert to submit to a paternity test."

"You think he would stoop that low?"

"Well, if my suspicions about Herman are true, there doesn't appear to be anything that would stop Gilbert when his butt's at risk. In the case with Herman, he needed to save the firm from a malpractice claim that would have been his fault. But here, his reputation's at stake, along with a large hunk of change he would have to pay to support his and Mary's son. The stakes are so much higher."

CHAPTER 11

"Don't tell me I ain't warned you."

"Mick called a couple of times and is anxious to speak to you. He couldn't get to you by your cell phone. Your battery dead?" my wife Theresa says as soon as I walk in the door after my visit with Molly in Glen Ridge.

"It's a long story, but I'll call him now, before he comes here bothering us."

"Francesca told me you and he had a big fight the other day. You pissed him off so much that he got up and ran out of your office."

"Yeah, but Mick and I are like brothers. We can have a huge fight—really curse and scream at each other—but then no apology's needed and we continue as if nothing had happened between us."

"I certainly hope so. Mick may be rough around the edges, but he such a solid person. I don't want you to hurt his feelings or ruin your relationship with him."

◆

THERESA AND MICK are staunch allies. This was in large part due to their like-mindedness but also due to Mick's sticking up for her when I first started to date her and my mother opposed our relationship. Theresa is Chinese; she immigrated to the States in her early twenties.

My mother decreed, "No, you must marry a nice Italian girl."

We had fights. I was outraged. I loved Theresa who is as sweet as can be with a charming personality and such a luminous smile. Mick was also taken by her. After their first meeting, he told me, "You better not let this one get away. She's real special, one of a kind."

I informed Mick about the problems I was having with my mother. He told me to stand back and let him work on her.

A few days later, Mick comes to see me.

"You ain't got nuttin' to worry about. Things are gonna work out between Theresa and your mom," Mick said.

"How the hell you pull this off?"

"Al, Al. As smart and as educated as you are, or you think you are, you sometimes don't listen when peoples talk to you. With your mom, you hear the words she says, but you ain't understood what she's sayin'."

"What are you talking about, Mick? Her precise words were 'you must marry a nice Italian girl.' How could anybody possibly misinterpret that?"

"Nope, that ain't what she's sayin'. Actually, I found out she had no friggin' clue about what's really botherin' her about Theresa.

"What she's really sayin' is, in the words of one of 'em songs in your mom's favorite movie, *Yankee Doodle Dandy*—you know about that guy George M. Cohan— she wants a 'gal just like the gal that married dear old dad.' She wants you to marry a dame that's just like her, with 'em traditional Italian family values.

"Once I know what's goin' on, I says to her, 'Listen to me, Auntie, there ain't no more Italian girls like you. The Italian girls here in Brooklyn, this whole country—and even in the old country, I'm told—ain't no longer into traditional family values; you know, willing to devote 'emselves to cook for the family and stay home to take care of the kids. Now they're into nice clothes, fancy cars, don't wanna do any housework, can't cook for shit, and that's the sad story nowadays.

"She thinks about it. Thinks about your sisters, our cousins, the girls in the neighborhood, what she hears from the relatives on the other side. And she sighs. She sees I ain't bullshittin' her and I'm tellin' her the God-honest truth.

"Then, I says to her, 'Auntie, I know Theresa. I talk a lot with her and watch how she treats Al, you, me and other people. From what I see, she got 'em traditional family values, same as you.' I says to her, 'Listen to me and do yourself a favor. You ain't want to create problems between you and Al. It's a sin for a mother and son not to get along.' I told her that you gonna do what you're gonna do, and it's much, much better if she's at peace with whatever you decide, especially when it comes to choosin' a wife.

"I says give Theresa a chance and if she ain't pass the test, I guaranteed to her that I'd get you to dump her. I tell her to talk to Theresa, watch her. See how Theresa behaves with others, like kids and old folks. See what she does at the Sunday dinner table; does she get up to help without askin' or bein' asked; or does she just offer to help, knowin' you gonna say no? Does she find out what you like and buy it for you? I let your moms know that from what I sees, Theresa's gonna make a wonderful daughter-in-law, who will be respectful and carin'. Just like old school Italians."

Theresa would pass all the tests. We married with my mother's blessing and her relationship with Theresa blossomed over the years. Theresa would never visit empty-handed; she would buy for my mom the things she liked. Theresa would call her every so often to check on her. They would often go to church together. If my mother seemed sad, Theresa would go over to cheer her up. When a friend of my mother's died, Theresa would go over to recite the rosary with her to pray for the repose of the friend's soul. In time, my mother would tell my sisters, her daughters, how much happier she would be if they were more like Theresa.

◆

I ASSURE THERESA, "It will be fine. Don't worry."

I call him. "Mick, what's up? Hear you looking for me?"

"Listen, asshole, don't play cute with me. Been tryin' you on your cell, hadda bother Theresa who knows how many times. What the fuck you up to with this here cloak-and-dagger shit?"

"Don't know what you're talking about, Mick."

"*Facimm*! You really think I'm dumb!"

"Mick, don't start with that crap!"

"Listen, I run into Sammy and he says he seen you today. I say, yeah? where? He tells me you called him, had him pick you up in the parkin' garage of your folks' place and then drive you to Penn Station so you can take a train someplace in godforsaken Jersey."

I think to myself: Thanks, Sammy, for keeping your promise to not tell Mick.

Mick continues, "And I screamed at him for chargin' you. He knows you always ride free with us."

"Mick, you can't fault him for that. I insisted he take the payment."

"He never even shudda told you how much."

"He didn't. Before I called him for the ride, I called your dispatcher and asked what the fare would be to Penn Station from my parents' place. I knew he'd never have told me. I don't like you and your guys working for me for free."

"Fuck, that's the least of it. So, what's goin' on? You ain't sneakin' around on Theresa to the cheatin' side of town, are you? 'Cause if you are, I will put a stop to that so quick you won't know what the fuck kicked you between the legs."

"Mick, you know me better than that."

I could never be unfaithful to Theresa, an exceptional soul mate, whose faithfulness was extraordinary, and it was impossible for me to be anything but totally devoted to her.

"I do, but one never knows. What they say, calm water has big undertow?"

"No. It's still water runs deep. Besides, you are not one to question anyone's virtue."

"Hey, what the fuck you talkin' about? I'm a million times more virtuous than you."

"Mick, how can you possibly say that? You, who used to run with whores, who would engage in sex like it was a handshake, and who used to say the most chauvinistic things about women."

"Well, you listen to me real good. You ever resisted the charms of a truly voluptuous woman, one who made your knees knock, and who's ready, willin' and able to get it on with you?"

"Ah, no, not really."

"Well, til that happens, shut your big trap. Only then you gonna know if you be virtuous. I've resisted, and while God knows I ain't no candidate for sainthood, I done the right thing and resisted the dirty deed despite opportunity that would've gotten the better of mere mortals, like you.

"I gotta say though, Al, what you says there about me and the ladies used to be true, and you don't know the half of it.

"But you don't think I cudda learned things and change, do you? Listen here. There was this kid that worked for me, Louie Romero. I don't know, maybe ten or twelve years ago, Louie gets in trouble that lands his butt in prison upstate. His wife, Barbara, and him have this little girl, hadda be maybe four then. She is the sweetest little girl, named Audrey. They ain't got nobody they know or could trust to watch the kid when Barbara went to visit Louie in the clink. So, I'd watch and play with this little girl. You know, go to the park, ice cream parlor, movies, all 'em things that the little kids like. And we become great pals. To this very day, she calls me 'Uncle Mickey' and even after Louie gets out, we stay in touch. I go see her around the holidays, bring her gifts. I get invited to her school stuff, you know, plays, graduation ceremonies—the whole thing. You'd think I'm her grandfather. That's the kind of deal she and I got goin'.

"So, this sweet girl becomes a young lady and starts lookin' like a grown woman. I says to myself, 'Shit, Mick, you ain't want nobody to think about your Audrey or treat her the way you treated the broads you been with.' This got me thinkin' about how terrible I been with 'em broads. After that, I no longer talk about women or treat 'em the same way. I start to deal with the ladies the way I want guys to treat my Audrey, 'cause if I find out that anyone treats her like I used to treat 'em broads, I'll go over the top to teach 'em a lesson they ain't never gonna forget."

I say, "This opened your eyes, heh?"

"Yep, it sure did," Mick responds. "But, I'm havin' a hell of a time overcomin' my rep. None of 'em better ladies wanna have anythin' to do with me. Even you, my own flesh and blood, ain't know about how I changed."

"Sorry, Mick. Actually, Theresa told me that you changed for the better regarding women, but I thought she was just sticking up for you like she usually does."

"Listen, Al, don't be an asshole. Listen to your wife. She knows what the fuck she's talkin' about, just like me. Your problem is you think smarts only comes from books."

"Mick, let's not go there."

"Okay, Al.

"Anyways, you distracted me from why I gotta talk to you. What the fuck's up? Do I gotta pull teeth to get it outa you? Whatcha done today gotta do with Mary and that scumbag Gilbert."

"Mick, that is not the only matter I am working on."

"I know that. I ain't dumb. But what's got you sneakin' into stinkin' Jersey?"

"I'd rather not say."

"Listen, Al. If you don't want me to smack it outa you, you'd better spill it, 'cause I ain't takin' any more disrespectin' shit from you."

"Mick, I told you I need to maintain absolute and independent control over all my matters and that includes this thing with Mary and Gilbert. I can't let it get out of control because of a loose cannon. Gilbert and Stillman will use that against me and it will only screw up Mary's chances."

"So, you rat bastard, this secret trip to Jersey is about Mary. Good thing you there and me here. I'd really give you a good smack."

"Mick, I'm an adult, not a kid."

"Well, act like one."

"Fuck you, Mick. You know I'm under no obligation to tell you anything."

"Al, not for nuttin' but I can't understand why the fuck you ain't willin' to trust me. I'll never, repeat, never, there ain't no fuckin' way in hell that I could, even if I tried, do anything to hurt you."

"Mick, I am afraid that in your zeal you will overstep your bounds and make it possible for Gilbert's team to claim some ethical breach on my side. Listen, even if there isn't, if there is the slightest appearance of a possible breach, they will milk it for all it's worth and, even if you and I are ultimately exonerated, something like that may give them the upper hand and screw everything up.

"This is not the same as the bribery allegation involving the city surveyor. There were no third parties involved there like there are here."

"Listen, Al, for the millionth friggin' time, you can't wait for these crooks to make the first fuckin' move. You gotta anticipate and be, what's that word … proactive, that's it. You gotta be proactive and beat 'em to the punch. Otherwise, you'll be crushed and can't do squat. Then, Mary's really screwed."

"Mick, I fully appreciate that I need to be extremely careful in my dealings with Gilbert. In fact, I went to Jersey at the request of a former colleague at G&A who now works at Joan's firm, who overheard something she wanted to bring to my attention. She also needed to alert me about something terrible Gilbert had done in the past."

"This person works for Gilbert's friend Joan? And you trust her?"

"Yes, I do, 100 percent. Knowing Gilbert the way she does, it was at her insistence that I sneak into Jersey by train so she and I could meet secretly."

"Well, what she hafta say?"

I fill Mick in about what the associate had said under his breath at the end of my meeting with Gilbert and Stillman and how they slammed him. I also told him the Herman story and Molly's advice to be super vigilant because who knows what Gilbert would resort to here where it's a personal matter that would hit Gilbert's pocket, his reputation, and his career.

"So, Al, with all that Gilbert has at stake, the legal shit is only a small part of the whole thing. Just exactly like I told you the other day when you threw me outa your office."

"Wait, hold it there. I did not and would never throw you out of my office."

"When you tell me that I ain't welcome to help, you're tellin' me to get the hell out."

"Mick ..."

"Forget it for now. So, now this woman tells you how nuts Gilbert is. It ain't nuttin' for him to ruin this attorney Herman so Gilbert don't gotta deal with a malpractice claim that'd be paid by the firm or its insurance company, right?"

"Yes, but by the firm, because Gilbert refused to make a claim against the firm's malpractice policy to avoid premiums being increased."

"So the fuck what? That ain't gonna come from Gilbert's pocket. This Mary business is personal to Gilbert. The Herman situation ain't, and he had the guy thrown in jail and screwed up his life. So, what the fuck you think he's gonna do to you so he ain't gotta deal with the embarrassment, the ruined career, yada yada that's gonna happen 'cause of Mary's case?"

"Mick, I understand all that, but I still need to be in total and complete control."

"Al, doncha be gettin' metaphysical on me. This is all intellectual bullshit that you're worried about. Gilbert's gonna be takin' it to the streets. That's the place where the fight's gonna happen, and your law, your legal procedure, your ethics ain't gonna protect you from the shit that's gonna be happenin' to you and Mary. The streets are my turf. I know what to do, how to handle whatever shit that's thrown at us. You don't, and you makin' a major, stupid mistake and'll be lettin' Mary down big time, if you're ain't gonna let me work with you.

"Ain't you see the type of scumbag we're up against?"

"We?"

"I'm gonna add that to the list of things I'm gonna let ride for now. This motherfucker and his goons, and I'm talkin' about his big shit attorneys too, are gonna attack and we don't know how 'til it happens—or more like after it's already done—'cause it's happenin' and we ain't even realize it's happenin' and that he's behind it. That's why we gotta be aggressive in our defense, to check out every possible angle of attack and meet it head on."

I say, "But I need to know what you propose to do and approve it before you do anything."

"We ain't got that kinda luxury most times. To find you, let you know what's happenin', give you time to debate with yourself what to do, discuss options, and then decide. Too late. Gotta act fast and act forcefully. Ain't always be neat and tidy, may hafta adjust and revise, but this'll always be on the fly. I gotta do what I gotta do, and I gotta use my gut in decidin' what and how to deal with shit on the spot."

"That's the problem, Mick. I'm ultimately responsible for what happens and can be sanctioned for not being in control, even if the results are good."

"Look. You gotta make up your mind. Who we tryin' to help? Mary or your reputation? If Mary's case ain't worth takin' some risks, then fuck it. Go to a monastery, say your prayers and you'll stay nice and clean. But realize who you're up against and be prepared to take this dirty-no-good-motherfucker and his scoundrels down. Or do your nice and neat by-the-books lawyer thing, then chalk up the loss to you-tried-your-best-but-lost, 'cause all lawyers win some and lose some, and go on with your nice tidy fuckin' life.

"But remember, Gilbert ain't only fightin' Mary, he's fightin' you, too. You're a target. Remember whatcha just told me about what he did to that poor guy Herman. Herman never knew what the fuck hit him. But *you* know real, real good that you gotta be on the lookout and gotta be ready for anythin' and everythin'. That's why you gotta have me to deal with the street stuff, while you concentrate on whatcha do best, the legal mumbo jumbo. We'll work together. Let me know whatcha up to, who you're dealin' with. That gives me an idea of what I gotta do And then I gotta keep you in the know of what I'm doin' and what I am findin' out. We gotta work like a team, but I can't always wait for your permission to do what I gotta do to help you and Mary. You gotta trust me that I'll do my best to help and do nuttin' to hurt you in any way. And all this goes for my guys too who'll be workin' with me."

I say, "I have enough problems not knowing what you are doing every step of the way. With others who I don't even know and have no control over added to the mix, my concerns are multiplied.

"Mick, if I need you, I will let you know what exactly I need you to do. But at this moment, I must go it alone, keeping my eyes and ears alert for any Herman-like moves on Gilbert's part. Once I learn something's in play—or even sense it— I will ask for your help. And I will dictate the help that I need from you. Before that, it is in Mary's and Roger's best interests if you keep your distance and wait for my call."

"Al, I give you all my reasons and you still spit in my face. Again, you're my cuz and I don't want anythin' to come between us. But, I gotta say over and over again, 'til I'm absolutely blue in the friggin' face, you're makin' a very big mistake and settin' up yourself and Mary and her little boy for disaster. You ain't appreciatin' the stakes. That kid'll never be taken care of the right way, Mary's life'll be wrecked, and your career as a lawyer'll be flushed down the toilet.

"Okay, you can't trust me. Fine, just don't tell me I ain't warned you. Good night, you asshole."

As soon as Mick hangs up, I suddenly remember Peg's call from the other night. I had totally blocked out that Gilbert somehow learned that Peg and I had been talking and forbade her to talk to me, or risk losing the chief clerk post. A feeling of dread comes over me, and I wonder if I am terribly misguided not to enlist Mick's assistance.

CHAPTER 12

"That's about all I can tell you."

THE METAL DOOR clangs shut behind me.

"Counselor, meet your roommate. They call him 'VD'," the guard says and chuckles.

I gulp, start to sweat. My bowels churn.

"VD?" I ask.

"Yep, that's right, VD."

Having closed and locked the door to the jail cell into which he led me, the corrections officer takes off.

As he walks away, I become aware of inmates in surrounding cells whooping and hollering, having a good time. Apparently, at my expense.

Out of the tumult, I hear, "Tonight's gonna be your honeymoon, white man!"

With me in the cell is a huge, muscular black man.

I could just barely say, "Hello. My name's Al," and nervously extend my hand.

The fellow shakes my hand and says, "Don't listen to that asshole. My name is Vernon Daniels. You call me Vernon. And don't be bothered by all that noise. Ain't nothing gonna happen between us."

I say, "Thank you very much, Mr. Daniels."

"Listen, it's Vernon. That guard don't know you're Mick Forte's cousin. Another officer passed on word to me from my man Malcolm and told me Malcolm ain't want nobody to mess with you here."

"Who's Malcolm and what's this about my cousin Mick?"

"Man, ain't you knowin' about your own cousin? He was in this here joint years ago with Malcolm and did Malcolm a solid, even though Mick's I-talian and Malcolm was the leader of the brothers. Malcolm was raised by his grandma and they were gonna put her out. Mick got his people to move her to a place in one of his buildings and they made sure she be took care of good."

"Oh. Mick never told me about that. And I never heard of Malcolm."

"Ain't you got a cousin named Eli?"

"No, no, that's Mick's cousin on his mother's side. Eli Ativa."

"Well, if you seen him, you know he a chubby little guy, but I was shocked at how athletic he be. And he gotta be over fifty."

"I did hear that he's a phenomenal basketball player. Also heard it almost got him into some trouble."

"You right about that. I know, 'cause I was there and got him outa what cudda been a hellava mess."

"Yeah. I heard. Mick told me that he and some fellow got to the basketball court just before a riot broke out."

"I was that fellow. This Eli really frustrated this other brother he played against. I hear he shut him down completely, really made the brother look real bad. Then Eli scores the winning basket by knocking it in with a soccer-like header. I seen it. Mick too. The man Eli was covering then called him out and Eli did this dumb-lookin' boxin' move and knocked the man to his ass with one punch."

"Yeah. Mick said Eli developed some move at a boxing gym. Said it was the 'Eli Shuffle'."

"Real funny shit. But he embarrassed this brother so in front of all these other brothers that the embarrassed brother hadda save face, and all 'em brothers brought out their weapons and wudda done Eli in but good, except Mick and me then stepped in and stopped it. You see, brothers don't like to be showed up. It makes 'em real mad. And if it's by a middle-aged, short, pudgy white man with glasses, no telling what they do. He sure damn lucky me and Mick was there."

"How did you two manage to prevent something bad from happening?"

"Well, 'em all knows Malcolm and knows that I be one of Malcolm's main men. So, I tells 'em all that Mick and Eli are friends of Malcolm and me and that now that they knows that, they also knows that to mess with a friend of Malcolm and me is to mess with Malcolm and me, and they knows what happens to those who mess with Malcolm and me."

"Wow."

"With that, everyone chilled, forgot about the negative shit, and peace ruled."

"Amazing."

"That's true. Anyways, now that you know how tight Malcolm and Mick be, they both got each other's back. So, they's got you covered too. Now, you just got here so I ain't got the full story about you, could only guess that somehow word got to Malcolm and through connections Malcolm has here, word got to me.

"And, they tells me you be a lawyer. That right?"

"Yes."

"Then what the fuck brings you here?"

"Excellent question. I am in my office working away this afternoon. The next thing I know court officers come barging in with an arrest warrant and whisk me over here. My assistant must have gotten word to Mick, and from what you say, he must have contacted Malcolm. But that's about all I can tell you now, except it must relate to a particular case I'm handling. I suppose Mick will be getting to the bottom of it and I'll know more tomorrow."

CHAPTER 13

"Let this mess be a lesson to you."

"You know, if you had only let your cousin help you, you wouldn't be in jail now."

"Theresa, what are you talking about?"

"You still don't know what you're doing here, do you?"

"No clear idea at all, except that it must have to do with the confidentiality order of that defamation case."

"Well, Mick tells me that if you weren't treating Mary's case so top secret, you'd be home relaxing this weekend and not wasting your time among the dregs of society."

"Theresa, please, I'm stressed enough!"

"My point, Al, is that if Mick knew about the defamation case and which judge has it, he would have put his ear to the ground and would have found out about the arrest warrant from his court officer contacts. So, instead of your ass being hauled into jail yesterday, Mick would have gotten your arrest delayed and hid you until Richie Abbatello could get it quashed."

Richie Abbatello is Mick's criminal defense attorney.

"And why are you in jail? Because someone called a reporter about Mary's case. Then the reporter called Gilbert's attorney, and he contacted the judge, and the judge issued the arrest warrant and ordered the court officers to arrest you immediately and haul your ass over here."

"Wait, wait, but I did not call any reporter."

"I have no doubt you didn't. You are very obedient and would never disobey a restraining order to keep your mouth shut. Mick says they set you up and that it has only just begun.

"Mick didn't come with me. Besides being real pissed at you, he's working on finding out who did contact the reporter. Richie needs this info, too, so he has the necessary ammo to get you out of here.

"And how many times do I have to tell you that you let your stupid pride blind you. When are you going to learn that you only know the law and only have book smarts? That's not enough. You need street smarts too, like Mick. Since you don't have street smarts, you need Mick on your team.

"In the meantime, Mick says to tell you to enjoy the prison chow and make sure you stay close to VD, whoever or whatever that is, when you take your showers, whatever that's supposed to mean.

"Richie will come to see you later. He needs to make some calls and get an update from Mick before he heads over here.

"And let this mess be a lesson to you."

CHAPTER 14

"They're out to get you. There is no doubt about it."

"LOOKS TO ME they're out to get you."

Richie Abbatello is the only one of Mick's friends growing up who became an attorney. He built up an impressive criminal defense practice in large part because of ties to guys from the old neighborhood. And because he's smart and shrewd, diligent and tough, and honest, Richie is a good attorney to have when you're faced with the possibility of prison. He is Mick's criminal defense attorney and Mick refers him without reservations to anyone Mick likes.

Hence, Richie is sitting before me in the prison visitors' center.

"They must be out to get you. Mick has been working to figure out what happened. So far, this is what Mick learned: John Burke, a reporter in charge of the City Hall desk at the *Times*, gets a phone call and the caller says someone named Mary Woodley is going to sue Deputy Mayor Gilbert for child support for a son he fathered out of wedlock. Burke is also told that Mary retained Al Forte as her attorney and Gilbert retained some hotshot lawyer named Stillman to bring a defamation action against Mary and you. Burke says that the voice was strange. Sounded like a person trying to disguise his or her voice, like a woman trying to sound like a man.

"Burke told Mick that he called Stillman and somehow he's able to get this extremely hard-to-reach attorney on the phone and asks him to comment on this information about Gilbert and Mary. Stillman then conferences in Judge Joseph so he can hear what the reporter had to say. Did you also get a call?"

"No, no one called me and I learned about the call to the reporter only earlier today from my wife."

"Well, this asshole judge accuses you of violating the confidentiality order without a shred of evidence connecting you to the call. And he does it *ex parte*. Without your participating in the call, as you well know, his decision goes against fundamental jurisprudence. He issues an arrest warrant and orders the court officers to go to your office and bring you directly to jail. Which, as you know all too well, they did. And you did not even get to pass 'GO' or collect two hundred bucks.

"I want to know what judge treats an attorney like this? I hear Joseph was recently elevated to acting Supreme Court judge; I wouldn't be surprised if Gilbert had some say in that. Anyway, this schmuck refuses to talk to me because it's the weekend. He doesn't care he has a brother attorney sitting in this hell of a jail. Luckily, I know the Administrative Judge, and he's pissed that his colleague has an attorney rotting in jail based on zilch. While he doesn't want to nix the other judge's order, over well-respected protocol, he got asshole Joseph on the phone and reamed him out good and told him that he had better grant me an emergency hearing the second I appear in his courtroom on Monday. And to also make sure you get out of jail the nanosecond he grants my *habeas* petition.

"Al, you gotta watch yourself with these people. They're out to get you. There's no doubt about it.

"Right now, Mick is digging deeper into the phone call. Burke gave him the phone number off his caller ID; now that I think of it, it's bizarre that the caller did not block the number from appearing—but that's not important right now.

"I'm waiting for more information from Mick, which I need for the papers I have to draft for Monday's hearing, so I can get you out of here.

"Tell me what gave rise to this confidentiality order. Mick told me about the pending paternity and child support proceeding you plan to bring on behalf of this Mary Woodley against Gilbert. I appreciate that that information is covered by the confidentiality order and I'll certainly comply with it. I don't want to create more problems. You have enough already."

"You can say that again. I know you don't want to keep me company here."

"You can bank on that. In fact, Burke got one of the *Times* attorneys on that conference call, and the *Times* agreed to comply with it, too. Apparently, Burke must have understood that this meant that the paper could not publish anything about the call, because he spoke freely with Mick, who had some previous connection with the guy—like he seems to have with almost everyone. But again, tell me what gave rise to that order."

"John Stillman of Adler & Stillman brought a defamation suit on Gilbert's behalf. My client, Mary Woodley, and I are defendants and the suit alleges that we have spread false rumors that Gilbert impregnated Mary and fathered a child. In place of Gilbert's name as plaintiff, Stillman used "John Doe" instead. Served with the summons and complaint was an Order to Show Cause why Gilbert's name shouldn't be kept anonymous and why the suit's file shouldn't be sealed. The Order to Show Cause also includes temporary restraining orders that prevent Mary and me from bringing a paternity and child support proceeding against Gilbert and from publicizing anything about this case. All these restrictions are in effect until a hearing scheduled for this coming Monday."

"That explains the timing for the call to the reporter and for your arrest and incarceration."

"I guess so."

"You can be sure of it."

I continue, "There is something else you should know about the defamation case. A few days after Mary and I were served, Judge Joseph's law secretary called me to tell me the judge wants to see both Stillman and me that afternoon in his chambers for an informal preliminary conference regarding the Order to Show Cause and its temporary restraining orders."

"That's unusual, isn't it?"

"I'm not a litigator and even I know that it's unusual, but when a judge calls, you jump. So, Stillman and I met with Judge Joseph that afternoon."

"What happened?"

"Judge starts off saying he wanted to warn me in particular that my client and I had better abide by the confidentiality requirements of the temporary restraining order. He said he wasn't as concerned about the restriction pertaining to bringing a paternity and child support proceeding in Family Court, as the clerk there was made aware of the prohibition. He said again that he wanted to put me, in particular, on notice that any violation of the confidentiality order will constitute contempt of court and subject the violating party to immediate arrest and incarceration, pending a subsequent hearing."

"That sounds quite strange."

"And I objected to it, especially because this was an informal conference without a record being made of what he is saying about contempt and arrest. And I questioned him as to why he assumed that I, or my client, would be the violating party. Judge Joseph said that the defense would benefit most by publicity of its claims, that some people hearing that Gilbert is accused of fathering a child out of wedlock will believe it regardless of the ultimate result of the litigation. And this would result in the real potential for irreparable harm to Gilbert's reputation and career.

"I told the judge that I have always respected orders of the court and will do everything in my power to ensure my client's claims are not made public to anyone and that anyone already aware of those claims will be informed to keep quiet, that it would hurt Mary if the confidentiality order was violated.

"Judge Joseph said that if word gets out, that it will be on my head, that there is no other effective way for him to enforce the order. To which I told the judge this absolutely requires that a record be made of all this, so it can be the basis of an appeal. The judge's response was, 'Request denied. See you both on the return date.'"

"What did Stillman say during all of this?"

"He simply stood there and smiled. The judge made his case for him and there was nothing he needed to add."

"You can say that again. Okay, I'll be back tomorrow to let you know what else Mick uncovers and to review my strategy with you."

"Okay."

"Before I leave, though, let me have a frank, attorney-to-attorney discussion with you about you and your cousin. As you know, Mick and I grew up together on the streets of what we called South Brooklyn, back in the day. Now, many of the guys we grew up with aspired to be part of the so-called Life. But as Mick would say, 'A lotta guys think they're called, but only a small number get chosen.' Those who didn't make the cut went into civil service, became cops, firemen, sanitation guys, bus drivers. Another thing Mick would say is 'You can take these guys outta the 'hood, but you can't take the 'hood outta 'em.' So, these guys stayed his friends, and Mick and they would help each other out whenever necessary. I'm the only one to become an attorney, but Mick is 100 percent correct that those ties bind just about forever.

"He's been my client over the years and I've seen how he has transformed himself. I don't think you're aware of certain important things about Mick, things that will make you view him differently and hopefully help you know that you can trust him and remove any concern that he would be a liability to you and your client's case.

"While Mick was powerless to thwart your arrest, once Francesca informed him that you were taken away, he immediately tapped his resources to learn where they brought you.

"This whole jail bullshit could have been avoided, because if the court officers knew that you and Mick were cousins, word would have gotten out and you would have been told to disappear 'til the end of the work day. That way, when the court officers came to your office to arrest you, all they could do was leave the warrant. Then Mick would have gotten me to quash the warrant first thing Monday without your ever coming close to this god-awful place.

"Not knowing your connection with Mick, they did what this idiot prick of a judge ordered and you know the rest.

"And thank God that Mick has the connections he has with the court officers, but especially this guy Malcolm. Your stay here would otherwise be unforgettably unpleasant."

I say, "Yeah. Tell me about this Malcolm."

"I represented Mick when he got sent away years ago. It was unfortunate that this deadbeat's cousin cop saw Mick smack the guy in the head with a bat. Mind you, though, Mick had good reason to do it—at least justifiable reasons as far as he, me, and the guys on the street were concerned. This cocksucker was behind on his loan payments and giving Mick lip. Usually, Mick would let that shit slide, but this *disgraziada e merd* rented apartments to both his mother and his mistress in this building he owned, the same building that he put up as collateral to secure his loan from Mick. And he charged his mother *double* the legal rent so his *putan* could live in her apartment rent-free. That's what earned the prick the good whack in the head that Mick had every right to give him."

◆

SOMETIME LATER, I spoke to Mick about how he ended up in jail.

"Yeah, it was 'cause of that fuck Alfred Russo. Whata piece of shit! While I was away my foreclosure attorney followed my orders to foreclose on that prick, which we did. I wanted that property so bad that I hadda pony up some money over what was owed me to get it at the foreclosure auction. Once that property becomes mine, my landlord-tenant attorney had Russo's *goomah* evicted, tossed on her ass outa the place. We lowered Mrs. Russo's rent to the correct amount. She was so shocked and pleased.

"That *cavone* would only visit his ma for her to cook for him whenever he dropped by for a quickie with his *putan*, who would, of course, also freeload at those meals. He mooched on his own mother; never bought her nuttin' or helped her in any way. And once he ain't no longer owned that building and his whore got evicted, he don't even stop by to visit his mom once in a while. My crew's takin' good care of his mother, and she's a very happy lady now. Who the fuck needs a dick of a son like that asshole?"

◆

Richie continues, "Anyway, this gets Mick sent away for a year. Now, as I said, he grew up with plenty of corrections officers. And there were plenty of his *paisans* in the clink too. So, he's got his back well covered. But in his own way Mick is forward thinking, ahead of his time. You must have heard what he did for Malcolm's grandma. That endeared Mick to the head of the prison's black faction. Mick similarly saved from eviction the mother of Pedro Ramos, who headed the Latino faction. Mick is now the prince of the prison. Not only that: He left here with strong allies and alliances for life—the benefits of which saved your butt now and for which you really gotta get on your knees and kiss Mick's feet.

"And, you must understand, it goes even further. Mick has ongoing dealings with both Malcolm and Pedro. Some of those dealings are how Mick staffs his legitimate businesses, like the property management and car service operations. He should get a civic award too, because he accepts referrals from Malcolm and Pedro for guys coming out of prison who want to go straight and would not otherwise be given a solid chance to get a job. And it has worked so well for Mick and from what Mick says, it's a two-way street, all three of them have reaped benefits from these alliances.

"Once he learned you were here, he called Malcolm and Pedro to discuss whom to contact among their corrections officer contacts to make sure you are kept safe from the inmate scum. The officer who took you to the cell wasn't in the Mick sphere of influence, but his supervisor is and he followed Malcolm's suggestion to bunk you with Vernon Daniels. Vernon's big and frightening looking, which would lead the casual observer to believe you weren't being treated with kid gloves. In truth, Vernon is a prince of a fellow, who got sent back to jail by a dick of a parole officer. I'll be getting him out soon, but we all agree we wouldn't get him out before you are released.

"Word's also being spread among the wiseguy inmates, the black inmates allied with Malcolm and the Latino inmates allied with Pedro, to further ensure that you are kept safe. I've had other clients, never exposed to the hard life—in other words, soft like you, no offense intended—who ended up in prison, who aren't even touched physically or directly intimidated. The atmosphere alone of prison has deleterious effects on those not used to the streets. I keep a team of shrinks busy helping some of my clients overcome the traumatic experience of being in these god-awful places and mingling with the worst element of society.

"Because of Mick, you will be walking out of here whole. Take advantage and get some rest for the long haul ahead of you."

I ask Richie, "Can you have someone bring me some of my files, so I can get some work done while I'm here?"

"No. There are limits. We must avoid your being treated so different that it draws attention. We're concerned about some of the supervisors and especially concerned about the so-called suits, the higher-level bosses, some of whom are political appointees.

"Anyway, Mick is sure that this is a move by Gilbert and Stillman. He thinks it's to shake you up at the start, mostly, expecting that your prison stay will frighten you and either render you incapable of proceeding or give you pause and weaken your resolve.

"Once they realize that this didn't accomplish the desired result, you can be sure they'll ramp it up. And my advice to you is let Mick loose. You desperately need his help or you will be at a terrible disadvantage and be a disservice to your client.

"And I know about that thing with the city surveyor. All I can say is, shit happens. The important thing is what happens at the end of the day and Mick wasn't even arrested and you weren't disciplined at all.

"Unless you want to operate in some ivory tower, where real life can't touch you, you cannot expect that you won't be hitting bumps along the way. That's life. And since you agreed to bring a case for your client against these scumbags, you owe it to her to use all the tools at your disposal to help her.

"Your cousin may not have much formal education, but he's real sharp, a good judge of character, trustworthy, and he knows how to get things done. He's got a graduate degree from the streets. Do not underestimate him. Understand that he can be fully trusted. Just don't piss him off."

I reply, "I have a lot to consider and I'll certainly think about all this."

"Just don't be such a straight arrow. You're in a fight with dicks who fight dirty. Doesn't mean you must fight dirty too, but you do have to be prepared for it, find out what's coming, and defend yourself and your client. And you're more the target. Once they take you out, she's isolated and can't do a thing to defend herself and assert her rights.

"One last thing and I'll leave you alone. Your cousin has extraordinary persuasive powers. Let me give you a screwball example and I swear I saw this with my own eyes."

I say, "Okay, go ahead."

"One spring, I had to stay with Mick for a couple of weeks while my wife and I were working through some issues. You know, in the neighborhood at the start of spring, ants suddenly appear, first in the kitchen and then all over the house. You must spray and spray until they stop coming. Well, your cousin stopped spraying a while ago. And he says he never calls an exterminator for any insects or rodents, nor does he set any traps or do anything like that."

I say, "Wait, wait, wait. He must do something. Ants will overrun your kitchen, swarm the rest of your house, and drive you out of your mind."

"You're right, but listen to this. What Mick does, he talks to them and dares them. When he sees the first ants, he kills them. Then he talks to wherever they came from and says, 'Hey, youse are welcome into my house. Butcha gotta know if I sees any of youse, I'm gonna kill youse. So, if youse wanna live, get the fuck outa my house and go someplace else. If youse don't think I'm gonna do it, then try me, 'cause if I see any of youse, youse're dead!'

"Believe it or not, with that speech, they go. You see no more.

"And Mick says it works for mice and rats too. If he sees any evidence of those rodents, droppings or gnawed-through bags or whatnot, or if he sees any as they run and hide, he gives them the speech and they're gone.

"He says he even has a policy for water bugs. He allows them to run free in the cellar, but tells them if they set foot—or whatever you call those things they crawl on— out of the cellar, and especially in the apartment, they are dead. He saw one just outside the cellar door and stomped it, then went into the cellar and told the others what he just did to reinforce to them the line that separates life from death.

"So, you see, even bugs obey him."

I'm speechless. All I could do is shake my head in astonishment.

"Now, you may want to try this approach in your house. If you do, I hope you're more successful than me when I tried. My attempt failed miserably and my house became so overwhelmed with those fuckin' critters, I had to spend a small fortune to get an exterminator to bring them under control.

"Anyway, sleep on what I told you about Mick and I'll be back tomorrow to update you on what else Mick finds out."

CHAPTER 15

"A whole lotta shakin' goin' on."

RICHIE ARRIVES THAT Sunday right after lunch.

"Mick's covered a lot of ground. He told me, 'There's a whole lotta shakin' goin' on.'"

"Okay, let's hear it, Rich."

"The phone that made the call is one of those disposable, burner phones. At first Mick's puzzled, like me, as to why the caller did not arrange to block the phone number from appearing on the reporter's caller ID. Most pros don't want their phones to be traced. By making the phone number known increases the possibility of it getting tracked."

"Yeah, that's odd. You think someone unsophisticated made the call?"

"Mick and I chewed over that and we conclude it was done that way intentionally, to throw everyone off the caller's trail by giving the impression that a non-pro was involved. We would expect that Gilbert and Stillman would only engage sophisticated pros. If a non-pro was involved that would deflect suspicion from them."

"I can see that."

"Besides, Mick is pretty sure that phone's been disposed of. So, whatever the truth may be, it's now likely buried with the phone. However, he's made note of the number just in case. You never know."

"Okay. Wise move."

"We learned a couple of other things about the phone. Based on the number, Mick has a guy who can tell you its manufacturer, who Mick somehow got hold of despite the weekend, and learned that the phone was sold at a kiosk at O'Hare Airport—you know, Chicago. This may explain why the phone number has a Chicago area code."

"Chicago? Well, I'm pretty sure Adler & Stillman has an office in Chicago"

"You're right. Mick checked. Interesting still, the call to the reporter was made from downtown Philly."

"Philadelphia? Don't tell me Adler has an office there too?"

"Bingo! Mick's on top of everything."

"So, what the hell is the significance of all that?"

"Your guess is as good as ours. As Mick said, things are 'shakin'.'"

"Yeah. You think that airport store has a record of the purchase and something that identifies the purchaser?"

"Yes and maybe. Unfortunately, the phone was purchased with cash. Had it been via credit card, the store would have the purchaser's name and would have photographed the person with one of those webcams. The store does have a record of the time of the purchase and Mick has an associate in Chicago going to the airport to see if he can somehow look at the airport security's surveillance video that covers the kiosk area around the time of purchase. We should know later if that leads anywhere.

"All this helps me with my *habeas* petition, as you were not out of town either when the phone was purchased in

Chicago a couple of weeks ago, and nor were you in Philly on Friday. I have the papers done and you will sign them now to swear to what I just said and that neither you nor anyone you know or at your direction made the call, which was a great shock and surprise to you. My papers will argue that they have no evidence whatsoever tying you to the call and that there is thus no basis for an arrest due to this mysterious violation of the confidentiality order. Too bad we have nothing right now that directly ties the call to Gilbert and Stillman. Anyway, I'll be in Judge Joseph's chambers at nine tomorrow morning and you should be home or at your desk by noon at the latest."

"This's great. I appreciate your work and, of course, Mick's efforts."

"In truth, this is mostly Mick. He has aggressively taken the lead."

"Well, I'm sure between him and Theresa, I will be eating lots of humble pie the next few days."

"I have more to tell you."

"Okay, let's hear."

"Mick took it upon himself to investigate that Herman matter."

"Why would he do that?"

"He said he wanted to see what there was to see."

"What the hell's he talking about?"

"Mick wants to understand how they operate, get into their heads some, if possible. Makes a ton of sense to me. You know, scout the enemy, learn how they maneuver, which may help you in your upcoming dealings with these folks."

"Okay, I guess that does makes some sense. He learn anything?"

"Some very interesting things."

"Let me hear."

"First, Mick got me the name of Herman's criminal defense attorney, Johnny Zachs. Fortunately, I know Johnny and spoke to him, and he told me that there were some real mysterious goings on with Herman. Johnny handled Herman's appeal and got Herman's sentence vacated and his law license reinstated, but he could do nothing about the psychological trauma that the whole mess inflicted on the poor guy.

"And if you remember what we discussed yesterday about the effects of jail on a person, Johnny told me that Herman got ruined by his stay in prison. Now, understand that the guards did their best to protect him. They understood something was off and that he had no business being there. So, they prevented any physical stuff and limited the verbal abuse. But you sit in this environment for months at a time unsure of your fate and fearing that all the work you did to build your practice and reputation is getting flushed down the toilet, not to mention where you stand with your wife and kids. You get killed, your heart, your mind, your spirit. It's a terrible thing. And when Herman is finally exonerated, he's a mere shell of his former self. Johnny lost touch with him and fears he may be confined to some mental institution somewhere. That's if he hasn't committed suicide."

"That's so messed up."

"Anyway, I passed Mick the information I got from Johnny, and Mick snooped around further. Here's what else he learned: First, no one knows who gave the unprecedented order to search all attorneys that day in court. And when I say 'no one knows' that includes the court officer in charge, some guy named Nelson. Second, Mick knows a narc who knows the narc who gave the preliminary opinion about the coke they found on Herman. That officer said that it was unusually pure, almost pristine cocaine, unlike the usual tainted quality you find on the streets. And lastly, the papers Herman submitted on the motion being argued were crap. The judge's law secretary was shocked by them, said it looked like the work of a first-year law student. They certainly were not the quality of the work product of an astute attorney like Herman."

"That just adds to the mystery, Richie. We know some things we didn't know before, but we still don't know the details of how they pulled it off."

"You're right, of course, but it tells us the lengths to which Gilbert will go when someone threatens him. It shows how devious and evil he can be. And as Mick informed me he already told you, how much more devious and ruinous will Gilbert be toward you and Mary, when it's his money and reputation at risk here, not some potential malpractice claim.

"So, in truth, we return to my original message: I do not care how good an attorney you are, you need backup. And Mick has the contacts and resources, and the backbone, that'll serve you well."

"Richie, with all due respect, I told you the concerns I have, of how Mick could hurt Mary's case—unintentionally, of course—but still impact it negatively. He can also do something that will hurt himself."

"Al, Mick is not the one to worry about. Gilbert and Stillman and their goons should be your first concern.

"What has happened to you this weekend is just the start of a strategy designed to wear you out, to weaken you, and to ultimately take you out. Mick told me that he told you they aim to prevent you even getting to first base, which means Gilbert would never even submit to a paternity test, which as you know without it you have no basis to maintain a child support proceeding.

"Mick and I think this first salvo is intended to give you a taste of what they can do and to test you. Test both your ability to counter it and your backbone and fortitude. To see how ready, willing, and able you really are."

I throw up my hands and say, "Okay, okay. I'll think this over carefully and decide what's the best way to proceed. Thanks, again, Rich. I greatly appreciate your help—Mick's too."

CHAPTER 16

"Time's a wastin'."

JUST AS RICHIE Abbatello predicted, I was released from prison and at my desk by noon on that Monday following my arrest.

Richie reported that Stillman was also at Judge Joseph's chambers by nine that morning. Richie argued to the judge that Stillman had no business there, as the matter was really between him and the district attorney. Stillman's client is not a party to the contempt of court proceeding.

Richie said Judge Joseph brushed everything aside and said he decided that there was no need to even read Richie's petition. The judge said I was lucky that the *Times* agreed to abide by the confidentiality order and there was no publicity. Under the circumstances, even if there were proof that I made the call, Joseph decided that the time I spent in jail was punishment and deterrence enough and ordered that I be released "forthwith." But Richie said that the judge instructed him to inform me that had the information conveyed during the call been publicized, he would have been extremely reluctant to release me so soon. Richie said he protested to Joseph that he had me between a rock and a hard place to take such a position without proof of my involvement, but the judge said to move on as the matter was now moot with my release.

Richie thinks the judge did this to get on the good side of the administrative judge, who assigns him cases. As an acting Supreme Court judge, he's beholden to a certain extent to the administrative judge, until he advances to full judgeship status.

Richie managed to get the return date for argument on the Order to Show Cause postponed to the following Monday. At first stupid Judge Joseph said adjournments could only be requested by the attorney of record, and that I risked a default if I did not get to the court by second call that morning. Richie told the judge that there was no way I could make second call, as I was still in the jail where that very same judge had ordered me. Before things got out of hand, Stillman made himself useful and simply consented to the adjournment.

So, after my adventure in jail, and my realization that the calls between Peggy Wells and me were somehow tracked by Gilbert's side, and after Theresa's and Rich's lectures, I now knew I had no choice but to adopt a different approach and team up with Mick. However, I did need to make sure that Mick knew he did not have carte blanche.

Around one in the afternoon, Mick stops by my office. I thank him for his assistance both in ensuring a pleasant stay in prison and in his investigations of the call to the reporter and of the Herman matter.

Then I say to him, "You've proven to me how invaluable you can be. I apologize for any bad feelings and I would like your assistance, but you must agree that this request is on a probationary basis. This means that I can withdraw it at any time, and if it's withdrawn, you have to stop whatever it is you're doing."

To which Mick says, "Fuck you, but if that gives you a hard-on and lets you save some face, okay. I don't really give a shit. What I care about are you, Mary, and Roger. I don't care that you ain't got no respect or confidence in me."

"Mick, stop it!"

"Okay. Screw it. End of discussion. Let's get down to business. Time's a wastin'.

"So, listen to me. I've been doin' a lotta thinkin'. We got a lotta plannin' to do. You gotta close your office early today, and you and Francesca gotta come to my place to meet with me. Mary too. I'll have one of my guys pick her and Roger up. Let's do it at 5:30, okay?"

"Yes, fine. 5:30 at your place."

We all arrive at Mick's office by 5:30 that afternoon and Mick leads us to a meeting room in the cellar below his so-called office, which consists of a square card table on which all kinds of papers and other objects are strewn haphazardly.

Once we get settled, Mary is the first to speak, "My God, Al, I only heard this morning about the call to the reporter and that they put you in jail. Those bastards!

"And now I see what Mick's been driving at and I'm happy you agreed to allow him to help."

I say, "What can I say? We live and we learn. Now, let's get down to work. Mick says he has some ideas. I've also been thinking a lot about next steps, but do go ahead, please, Mick."

"So, we now got an idea of what we gotta look forward to. Al's goin' to jail ain't have happened if only he'd listened to me, but I'm glad what I been sayin' has been learnt, even if it's the hard way.

"Anyways, that's done and we gotta move on. I got some ideas about what we gotta do, so our friends can't sneak up on us and surprise us again. We gotta track what they're plannin'."

"How are we going to do that, Mick?" I ask.

"Informants. Get persons behind enemy lines so we know what they gonna do before they do it. I already got somebody in Stillman's office."

I ask, "Someone in Stillman's office? Who can that possibly be?"

"Smitty."

"Smitty? Who's Smitty?"

"You know him."

"I know no one there named Smitty."

"Whatcha mean? Youse all met him. You, Mary—even Francesca."

Francesca says, "You're nuts, Mick."

"The guy who came to the office that brung you 'em papers. That black guy."

"You mean Bill? He's only a process server at Stillman. How do you know he knows what's going on over there and, more importantly, that we can trust him?"

"Well, first, I ain't never knew Smitty worked there. Just knew he worked for some lawyers. I saw him that day he come into and outa your office, Al. He sees me across the street havin' some coffee and comes over to say hi and talk some. He wondered if you and me are related."

"How do you know him? Through that Malcolm fellow? From your time in jail?"

"No, no. Smitty's not connected with Malcolm and never been to no jail. Smitty retired from military intelligence. He's totally straight. I knew his older brother, Matt. Matt was a hard dude, took book, was a shark, and didn't deal drugs, but he was an addict for a long time.

"I brokered peace between Matt and a coupla *paisans* and kept Matt from gettin' whacked and that got Matt to close his shop here and move to St. Louis. He got clean there but died of lung cancer about five years ago. I met Smitty at Matt's funeral. Matt told Smitty about me.

"Anyways, Smitty volunteered to help anyways he can. He hates the pricks he works for. Smitty says he hears all the shit that goes down at that office, and'll keep his eyes and ears open for anythin' that hasta do with Mary."

"You think he knows anything about the call to the reporter?"

"The first call I made was to Smitty about that. He says if he'd known anythin' like that was gonna happen, he wudda let me know pronto. But he heard nuttin' and even checked around and still came up with nuttin', except for things we already knew, like Stillman gettin' the call from the reporter and the conference call with the judge and you goin' to jail."

"How can you be really sure that we can rely on him for assistance? He couldn't find out anything about the call."

"We can rely on him, 'cause I say so. He couldn't find out anythin' about the call either 'cause there was nuttin' to find out or they're keepin' a tight lid on it. You can be sure that if there's anythin' that he can dig up, he will and he'll let me know about it."

"Okay, I guess we will have to settle for that. However, we must keep in mind that his alliance with us is no assurance that we will know everything that we need to know, that we'll also need to be alert independent of him."

"You took the words right outa my mouth, Al. Finally, somethin' we agree about. And also, we gotta remember that the dirty tricks might be done by Gilbert alone. Stillman may not wanna ruin his reputation. We'll see, but it's possible that Gilbert's doin' shit behind his lawyer's back.

"Fact is, Smitty says the firm is aggressive and tough, but as far as he knows they ain't done nuttin' criminal. Smitty says Stillman brags that Gilbert came to him, 'cause that fuck wanted an attorney who's tough but not sleazy, probably to make Gilbert look better. Smitty says Stillman likes to show off, he's pompous, but he won't do nuttin' dirty. It's good to know this, but it don't make no difference. We gotta watch Stillman like a hawk anyways.

"And one other thing about Smitty. His help to us gotta be top, top secret. That goes without havin' to say, right?"

All heads nod, even little Roger's.

"Next, let me say that I even got a possible informant in Gilbert's office, but I gotta talk about that person with Al first.

"We also gotta agree how we gonna act when it comes to Mary's case. I got some ideas about that too."

I say, "Go ahead. Let's hear what you have."

"We gonna be in covert operation mode. We don't want 'em to tap into our phones, hack our computers or e-mail accounts, and we don't want 'em to harass us in any way. So, whenever we talk about Mary's case by phone, we gotta be usin' the disposable phones I'll be handin' out. And those phones ain't gonna be used for no other purpose. Smitty'll be gettin' one of 'em phones, too."

I say, "Okay, what else do you recommend?"

"E-mail and word processin'. Julius, my IT guy, is gonna create an e-mail network that'll only include e-mails by Al, Francesca, Mary, and me for when we need to e-mail between each other about Mary's case. Also, each of us gonna have a special, single-purpose laptop to use to send those e-mails. And Francesca and Al'll use those laptops of theirs to prepare all court documents. Document sharin' is gonna happen by sendin' stuff through the secure e-mail account or by usin' zip drives. The laptops we'll have tomorrow.

"Everythin' about Mary's case—calls, documents, meetings—hafta be top secret. And with word processin', don't forget that Gilbert somehow screwed around with the court papers that that guy Herman prepared for his client. We gotta take these special, extra steps for the papers youse write up for Mary's case.

"And I'll cover the costs for the phones and laptops. After this is over, the phones and laptops are mine."

"That's reasonable and generous. Thanks, Mick. And these are all excellent suggestions. Anything else?"

"Yeah. For security reasons Mary and Roger gotta move into one of my buildings so me and my crew can keep an eye on 'em. Also, Jimmy's gonna hafta escort Francesca to and from work, whenever he can. If he can't, me or one of my guys'll do it."

I say, "Alright."

"Also, we gotta avoid public transportation and rely on my car service to get around, and any meetings about the case gotta happen here. We check this space for bugs on a regular basis."

I ask, "Why's that?"

"Oh, good question. Habit, I guess. Anyways, we gonna be needin' to do it now. They'll eventually know that somethin' is cookin' over here, but that's alright. Any trouble, I bring in Captain Luongo, good friend from the local precinct whose mother is one of my tenants, or Council Member Carlo Ruisi or Richie, whoever is right to solve the problem.

"Okay, a coupla other things. Security for the office. I'll have Joey my security guy look over your office space and see what he says about improvin' the locks and doors, about installin' some metal bars on the windows in the back, and about puttin' in the most advanced silent alarm system. Maybe a good idea to have a watchman overnight; stay outta sight in the back, surprise anyone who tries somethin' funny. Then, we need folks to do surveillance and stake-out work, that's sure to be needed. There's my people, and Malcolm and Pedro says they'd let us use some of their people too. I'll supervise alla that. That okay with you, Al? I promise to keep you in the know about what's happenin'."

"Please do and thanks, Mick."

"Yeah, sure. Now, even with everythin' we got planned, we ain't always gonna know when they're gonna try somethin' or know what to look out for, so we gotta keep our eyes and ears open at all times and stay on our toes."

"Understood. Thank you again very much, Mick. Given what transpired this past weekend, your proposals are well taken and I agree with them all and really appreciate the amount of thought you have given this."

Mick says, "Let's keep movin'. Ain't got no time for speeches."

"Okay. Now, Mary, you and Roger willin' to move?"

"Yes, but how much will the rent be?"

Mick replies, "Don't worry about that. This ain't goin' on forever."

Mary says, "Thank you very much, Mick."

I ask, "Francesca, sound alright to you?"

Francesca responds, "You betcha, Al, about office protocol and with Jimmy's schedule, he should be able to escort me to work and back home most days."

"Okay. We are going to need to do a lot of adjusting to implement these safeguarding protocols, but it will all be for the best in the end.

"Mick, I need to get home. We have some further planning to do. Let's talk tomorrow about that and about whom you recommend to be the informant in Gilbert's office."

Mick says, "Meet me here at ten, okay?"

"Yes, ten it is. Good. Good night everyone."

After some milling around, Mick lines up drivers to take everyone home.

CHAPTER 17

"We ain't got no other choice."

Mick usually sees things in black and white, absolutes.
There are no shades of gray as far as he's concerned. When
Mick makes a move he's pretty sure that it's the right way to
go and there is very little doubt in his mind. Simply stated,
Mick exudes confidence. So, it was somewhat of a surprise
for me to listen to what he had to say about this guy named
JBJ, Mick's candidate to be our informer in Gilbert's office.
The matter of JBJ was exceptional as far as Mick is con-
cerned, and if there wasn't so much at stake for Mary and
Roger, it would have made for a fascinating case study.

Mick informed me that JBJ's full name is Johnny Boy
Giambini, Junior, but everyone in the neighborhood calls
him JBJ. Family members call him Junior. Now that he is
an adult and working, he goes by John to outsiders.

"Al, you know the kinda guy I'm talkin' about. A lazy,
spoiled Italian mama's boy. All his life, and he's twenty-two
now, he's been a brat and a bully, but when someone gets
in his face, he backs down like the lousy punk he really is.
You know, he's just like that guy whose ass you kicked and
sent to the hospital. What's his name? Johnny Pinto, no?"

"Mick, first, you refer to Jackie—really 'Giacomo'—
Pintero, and I did not hurt him much and certainly did
not send him to any hospital."

"Then what the fuck happened between youse two."

"Okay, I'll make this quick.

"I must have been eleven or twelve, so in the seventh grade. Jackie was a year behind me. We were assigned to be altar boy partners and he was a royal pain in the ass. And a real punk, like you said; a lot of big talk but would always back down, but no one ever did anything and this made him bolder and a bigger annoyance.

"So, my patience with this *schmuck* is wearing thinner and thinner and reaches the breaking point one day when we're returning to the main church after serving at the chapel at the foot of President Street, you know, on the block that used to be 'Crazy' Joey Gallo's base of operations during his heyday."

"I know that better than you ever will."

"Anyway, we walk up my block of Carroll Street and Jackie begins to pick on little Lenny, the kid who lived across the street from me and who was probably seven or eight at the time. I tell Jackie to bug off and he tells me to either do something about it or shut up. Before I could react, he scoots off. It was then and there that I decide that I had to kick his ass.

"In those days, we had altar boy meetings every Saturday morning in the Rectory basement. I decide that I would beat Jackie up after that Saturday's meeting. During the meeting, I would look over at Jackie and make the meanest face I could …."

"That musta made him real scared. Did he pee his bloomers?"

"No and *sta zitt* and listen. He gives me a funny look that makes it clear he had no clue what I was trying to convey to him. He's equally clueless when I made a fist of one hand and pound it into the other hand."

"I'm shocked he ain't drop dead of fright at that scary sight."

"You want to shut up for a second? Anyway, as the meeting lets out, he runs out ahead of me. I go out and walk up to him. He says to me, 'Why you making faces at me?' I tell him, 'I've had it with your bullshit and I'm going to do something about the way you treated Lenny the other day.'"

"Did he start to cry and run away?"

I make believe Mick hadn't said anything.

"I then push him in the chest with both hands. Now, we are a good eight feet from the street. There is this tractor-trailer parked at the curb, and after I shove him, Jackie goes flying backward much faster and further than the push justified. I'm convinced he's faking it, to show that I was attacking him without notice and taking advantage of his inability to defend himself. Anyway, his forehead gently glances off the bottom edge of the side of the truck. He turns around with his hand on his forehead, crying, 'He made me hit my head, look at this blood!' The other guys step between us. Joey Amalfitano tells Jackie to stop being a baby, that his forehead is hardly scraped and there is barely any blood. After a minute or so, the commotion dies down, Jackie sneaks off and I head home with jealous thanks from several of the guys who wish they had gotten to Jackie first and who regret that I did not get to really kick his butt good."

"Wow. I'm surprised you didn't get arrested."

"Come on, stop already."

"So, what happened in school that Monday?"

"Well, nothing happens that Monday. In truth, what had happened on Saturday was so nothing that I didn't think anything of it. However, that Tuesday, another altar boy and I are assigned to a funeral. The procedure is for us to go to the principal's office to inform the principal's secretary that we are going to serve a funeral; we would then report back to the secretary upon our return. In any event, who should be in the principal's office at the very moment we are checking out, but Jackie Pintero and his mother."

"No shit."

"You said it. I almost drop a load right then and there, because that *stroonz* points at me and says to his mother in Italian: 'That's the one who hurt me!' Jackie and his family were recent immigrants and his mother spoke no English. So, first of all, on what had been barely a scrape now was a bandage that covers almost his entire forehead, and there is a nice red blotch oozing through the sucker, making it look like his whole forehead had been fucked up. Second, I am shitting in my pants, thinking of having to face my parents about this."

"So, how'dja weasel outa it?"

"I'm a real mess, fumbling and mumbling excitedly, 'It was an accident that he hurt his forehead and only a small part got hurt ... .' Well, the principal, Mother Gertrude, tells me to be quiet and tells Mrs. Pintero in Italian: 'I know this boy (pointing at me) and I know his family. He comes from a very good family and I have never had any problem with him. Your son, on the other hand, is always giving his teachers nothing but trouble. I do not know what happened to your son's head and I do not care. Even if this boy (pointing at me) did do something to your son, I have no doubt that your son deserved it. Now, until you manage to get your son to behave himself, do not expect me to clean up the messes he makes for himself with the other students. Now, go home and pray to God for the grace to figure out how to straighten your son out.' With that, she dismisses me to go to the funeral and that is the end of that."

"No shit. Didn't you realize that you cudda beat up anybody?"

"You know, that I had virtual freedom to do that never occurred to me back then. I even forgot about the whole incident for years afterward. Anyway, I probably could have gotten away with beating up a couple of other kids until Mother Gertrude finally caught on that I was taking advantage of having an unblemished reputation. But, then again, other than Pintero there really wasn't anyone else I wanted to thrash."

"That's one fine story. If that'd been me, that nun wudda bashed me but good, if I done somethin' or not, 'cause of my rep of bein' a thug.

"Anyways, JBJ ain't much different than that shithead Jackie Pintero."

"So, how does that make him a suitable candidate to be our informant in Gilbert's office?"

"Excellent question, counselor. It's another one of 'em 'lucky coincidences' we been talkin' about. We ain't gonna always be so lucky, so when we get one of 'em we gotta milk those mothers for all 'em's worth. That's really the only qualification this guy's got. Here he's sittin' right in Gilbert's office and there ain't nobody else available to us."

"Back up. How did he manage to work for Gilbert anyway?"

"You know Carlo Ruisi, the City Council Member for this district."

"Of course, and I know him personally, though we don't get much of a chance to chat these days."

"Well, the Giambini family been great supporters of Carlo since he started in politics, and they always get out the vote for him. So, even though he's a politician, and I ain't trust most politicians, Carlo's alright. He ain't that power hungry and looks like he works hard to help the people in the neighborhood. He's got a power base and political allies, but he uses 'em to do good things from what I know.

"Carlo's a power broker 'cause of helpin' to get the vote out for other candidates of the party too. He's tight with the mayor even, who owes Carlo, 'cause of Carlo's loyalty and ability to rally his people in the mayor's favor. So, this gets Carlo a number of patronage slots to fill. 'Cause of his ties with the Giambini's, one slot got reserved for JBJ and by pure luck that slot lands him in the Office of the First Deputy Mayor, where this punk has got the fancy title of Special Assistant to the First Deputy Mayor. A load of crap, if you ask me.

"So, that's where we find ourselves.

"Tonight, we'll meet with this Special Assistant at his house and talk things over with him to see if this JBJ's gonna help us get some idea of what his boss Gilbert's up to."

"You really think he can render any meaningful assistance."

"Ain't sure at all, but we ain't got no other choice."

"He may really screw things up for us."

"Ain't gonna disagree. While his mom spoiled the shit outa him, she is devoted and loyal to me, 'cause of the help I gave her family. And between her and me, we'll be on JBJ's butt to make sure he don't fuck up."

"You're right. We have no other choice and hopefully it helps some." I wasn't putting too much stock in this JBJ, but being able to get an inkling of what Gilbert is up to would be invaluable—if it does not backfire on us.

"Okay, you know where they live. Be there by eight. By then dinner's finished and we can spend some quality time with this JBJ, who just may turn out to be a whatchama-callit—a diamond in the rough." Mick's positive attitude counteracted to some extent the doubts I had about this JBJ fellow.

CHAPTER 18

"Here's JBJ."

MICK IS ALREADY there when I arrive at the Giambini residence.

"Al, thanks for joinin' us. I know you know Mrs. Giambini here. And this here's JBJ."

Slouching on a dining room chair is this skinny fellow with a blank, sullen stare and bored and distracted look. This is the person that earlier in the day Mick spent considerable time describing to me. I think to myself, "This is going to be mighty interesting."

We know that the less JBJ knows about our situation the better, so Mick and I simply tell JBJ that in order to help someone from the neighborhood we need him to get us certain information about Gilbert.

We ask JBJ what his daily duties are.

JBJ says, "I ain't tellin' youse fuckin' shit until youse tell me what the fuck's in it for me."

Mrs. Giambini gets up from her chair, dashes across the room to JBJ and gives him the traditional Italian mother's smack to the back of his head, causing his head to almost hit the table in front of him.

"Heh, ma, what the fu—!"

Mrs. Giambini screams, "*Scustamad e merd*!" Loosely translated, "You selfish shit!" but the way Italian mothers typically shout it makes one feel deeply ashamed and miniscule.

"Junior! When this man (pointing to Mick) says jump, you jump. When he says crawl, you crawl. And when he says nothing, you go to him and ask, 'What can I do for you to repay you for all the things you done for me and my family?' And besides the help he gave your father, your uncle, your aunt, don't forget who got you that lawyer when you got caught selling drugs in high school. He also stopped that *facimm* who let you buy liquor when you were only fifteen.

"And we don't even know all the people he talked to for you, for them to give you another chance even after all the bad stuff you done.

"'What's in it for me?' you ask. *Oo gotz*! You got the nerve to ask. Mick over here never asked that *disgraziada* question when *we* needed help. He did not have to lift a finger, but he did and he did and he did and he did. NOW, he asks for a little help and you act like he's asking you to sacrifice your life. *Va fa gool*!"

JBJ says, "Okay, okay, Ma, sorry, but I'm worried about this job. What if I get fired 'cause of what these guys want me to do?"

Mick jumps in, "JBJ, you got the job 'cause of Carlo. Carlo is term limited out at the end of next year. So, ain't no way you gonna be there long anyways. And I ain't never gonna ask you for help if I ain't gonna have your back if helpin' me hurts you. *Gabbish*?"

JBJ seems to get what Mick's saying and nods to show his assent.

"Now you're gonna tell us whatcha normally do at the office and we'll tell you how you can help. And during the time that we need your help, which'll be for a month or so and maybe longer, you ain't doin' nuttin' that'll get you fired and you ain't gonna quit either. *Gabbish?*"

Again, JBJ nods his head.

We learn that JBJ was basically a gofer for Gilbert. He would run both business and personal errands for him. His duties include reminding Gilbert of appointments on his calendar and keeping Gilbert's cell phone charged. His desk is located right outside Gilbert's office and the door to Gilbert's office is generally kept open, except for certain calls, when Gilbert would order JBJ to close the door. That demand is always given when Gilbert got calls from the mayor or Stillman, whom JBJ said is a "fuckin' snob."

We decide Mick would meet with JBJ every night either at his house or some other predesignated spot. Rather than trust JBJ with a disposable phone, he is given an 800 number to call Mick in the case of an emergency and or if there is information that needed to be imparted immediately.

The initial assignment we give JBJ is to make a note of any contacts or calls with the 312 area code on Gilbert's cell phone log. For the time being, we assume and hope that Gilbert would not use his work phone for his dirty tricks involving Mary.

We ask JBJ what would happen if someone noticed his looking closely at Gilbert's phone while it is being charged. He says, "They ain't gonna say shit, 'cause Gilbert has me programmin' his phone to add different apps and shit. And if he's got his door closed or is outa the office, I play all sorts of games and do other crap with his phone and everyone sees me do it and ain't gonna think nuttin' of it."

The following day, JBJ reported that as of the last time Gilbert's cell phone log was erased, which was a week ago and included the day of the call to the reporter that landed me in jail, there were no 312 numbers on it. Nor did the phone numbers of any of Gilbert's contacts have that area code.

JBJ did tell us the night we met that Gilbert was in Philadelphia the day of the call to the reporter, but that his train would have been in New Jersey at the time that call was made from downtown Philly. This meant that if Gilbert was truly on that train, Gilbert could not have made the call to the reporter, but we already assumed that Gilbert would have had one of his cronies make the call.

Mick would tell me later, "Jimmy Cavello's brother-in-law, Max, works for Amtrak. I'll get the ticket info from JBJ and have Max check to see if it was scanned by the conductor, so we know whether Gilbert was on that train. I once saved Max from gettin' his throat slit. He was in a bar he had no business bein' in. Lucky for him, I was walkin' by or it wudda been bye-bye for Maxie. The guy who was gonna cut Max is still singin' 'em high notes."

JBJ also told us that Gilbert was in Philadelphia supposedly to attend some conference. However, as JBJ overheard Gilbert tell some colleague over the phone, Gilbert had no intention to attend any of the conference. Instead, JBJ reported that Gilbert said, "In the immoral words of Mick Jagger, I am going there to 'make some girl'." Apparently, Gilbert's ulterior motive in being in Philly was to seduce some woman who was attending the conference. JBJ said that Gilbert was scheduled to stay in Philadelphia that Friday night and to return Saturday on a midafternoon train.

We instructed JBJ to see what he can learn about that lady. He told us that night that he was sure that Gilbert had gotten "lucky" with her, because on the Monday morning after the conference Gilbert came in, uncharacteristically, grinning from ear to ear.

JBJ said, "He's mad always. He ain't nuttin' but a mean prick."

Then added, "I know her name's Margaret."

I said, "Wait! That's his wife's name."

JBJ responded, "No! His wife's Margie and from the way he talks on the phone with this Margaret, ain't no fuckin' way in hell could she be his wife, 'cause he's always real nasty to his wife."

JBJ also told us that on the day I was released from jail, Gilbert was screaming at Stillman over the phone. Even with the door closed, JBJ heard Gilbert exclaim, 'Why the fuck did you let that cocksucking judge let him out of jail? I wanted him to stew there for at least a week!' and 'Who the fuck gave you permission to consent to an adjournment for that hearing! You're wimping out on me!'"

As we left this initial meeting with JBJ, I asked Mick what he had done for the Giambini family other than what Mrs. Giambini said about how he had helped JBJ.

Mick says, "JBJ's dad's name is John Giambini Senior, but for some reason everybody calls him Frank. Anyways, I helped the old man when he got sick. Had my guys get him to and from his doctors' appointments. When this one doctor wasn't payin' proper attention to him, I had a conversation with the doctor and adjusted his attitude toward Frank. And when I found out a male nurse mistreated Frank, Pedro had one of his guys make sure the nurse never made that mistake again.

"Then there's the uncle, one of 'em degenerate gamblers. Died without two pennies to his name. I made sure he had a proper wake and burial. His poor widow was left destitute. Rather than have her go to the poor house, I put her in one of my apartments and she's never been happier.

"Al, hear me out, 'cause this here too is a lesson for you, though I gotta say you already know this, proof bein' how you helpin' Mary and little Roger. Who knows, maybe this runs in our family? Anyways, if somebody needs help and I can help, I help 'em. If I need help and someone can help me, like JBJ now, I expect that they will help me. It ain't in any way even Stevens, 'cause that ain't how I like to be, but this is the way things is: We help each other anyways we can. Nobody keeps count who's done more for who. You never know whatcha'll need, when you'll need it, so it ain't the kinda thing you cudda keep track of anyways."

As we both go our separate ways, we both agree that this twerp JBJ just may turn out to be an ace up our sleeve.

CHAPTER 19

"We are here for both parties to make their arguments."

THE FOLLOWING MONDAY, Mary and I are in court for the hearing on the Order to Show Cause and its temporary restraining orders.

As the hearing is also governed by the confidentiality order, the courtroom is empty except for Stillman, Gilbert, Mary, me, the court stenographer, a court officer, the judge's law secretary, and Judge Joseph.

The transcript for the hearing reads in relevant part as follows:

JUDGE: "Okay. The attorneys for both parties having noted their respective appearances, let us proceed. This matter, a defamation suit, was accompanied by an Order to Show Cause demanding that the named defendants, Al Forte and Mary Woodley, show cause at this hearing why this suit's court file should not be sealed and why the name of the true plaintiff should not remain anonymous. Further, I imposed certain temporary restraining orders pending the results of this hearing, namely, that (i) all matters pertaining to this suit be kept strictly confidential, (ii) the paternity and child support claims of Ms. Woodley not be publicized, and (iii) the bringing of any suit with respect to those claims be prohibited.

"As we all know, someone violated the confidentiality portion of the temporary restraining orders by making a phone call to a reporter informing him of Ms. Woodley's claims and of this defamation suit. Based on that violation, Mr. Forte spent a weekend in jail.

"At this hearing, the defendants are to show why this suit's court file should not be sealed and why the plaintiff's true name should not be stated as an anonymous name in the caption of this case. So, Mr. Forte, the floor is yours."

FORTE: "Your Honor, before I address the issues at play, let me state for the record that my imprisonment was without a shred of evidence that I, Ms. Woodley, or anyone acting on our behalf had anything to do with the call. While Your Honor assumed that I violated the order, you did so after an *ex parte* call with plaintiff's counsel Mr. Stillman alone and I was not given an opportunity to be heard. It is beyond me why this Court did not consider the possibility that plaintiff was behind the call. I recognize that this is water under the bridge at this juncture, but I just want that to be duly noted."

JUDGE: "Well, it is now on the record for a case whose file just may well be sealed, for all the good it is going to do you. Anyway, stop wasting our time and get to the merits of this hearing, counselor."

FORTE: "We will consent to the sealing of the file and to the anonymous name in the caption, provided Deputy Mayor Gilbert submits to a paternity test."

JUDGE: "Mr. Forte, this is not a negotiating session where you agree to this in exchange for the other party doing that. We are here for both parties to make their arguments regarding the specific matters raised in the Order to Show Cause and for me to render a decision based on the legal merits of those arguments. Now, remember that and proceed."

FORTE: "Yes, Your Honor. With all due respect to the Court, I may be putting the cart before the horse, but we are just playing games here over trivial matters, where the crux of the defamation action is whether my client's claims are false and defamatory. The answer to that requires the Deputy Mayor to submit to a paternity test. We concede that his being tested must be confidential. If the test shows he is not the father, then damages would be the sole issue in this suit. Our position is that damages would be minimal, if any, given the sparse publicity of the alleged defamatory statements and also given that those claims are believed to be meritorious and made in good faith. On the other hand, if the paternity test shows that Gilbert is the father, then this defamation suit must be dismissed with prejudice, based on truth being an absolute defense as a matter of law, and Mary be permitted to petition Family Court for child support."

JUDGE: "You are correct, Mr. Forte, you have put the cart before the horse. We are not yet at the juncture where we get to the merits of the underlying case. Mr. Stillman, it is now your turn. Please proceed. More importantly, kindly address the issues."

STILLMAN: "Judge, it appears that my adversary does not care to contest the sealing of this case's file by the Court. Nor does he care to contest to my client's being named anonymously in the caption of this case. So, it appears that those issues are resolved."

JUDGE: "Mr. Stillman, excuse me for cutting you off, but they are not resolved unless I am satisfied there is good cause to do so, taking into account the interests of the public to know about this case, as well as the interests of the parties to this action. Please proceed."

STILLMAN: "As a matter of public policy and of principle, the claims against First Deputy Mayor Gilbert must not be exposed to the light of day, nor should he be required to submit to a paternity test, based on the unfounded claims of a deranged individual."

FORTE: "This is insulting. I object, Your Honor."

JUDGE: "Yes. The stenographer is to strike the words "of a deranged individual" from the record. Mr. Stillman, you have been doing this longer than I, and you should know better. I will not tolerate the gratuitous insulting of a party in this courtroom, even while closed to the public. That does not excuse the use of derogatory language. Now, apologize to Ms. Woodley and move on."

STILLMAN: "Sorry, Judge. Ms. Woodley, kindly accept my apology."

WOODLEY: "Accepted."

STILLMAN: "As I was saying, both public policy and principle require that those claims be proven before such claims against a public official can be made public. And, because Mr. Forte raised the issue, let me add that there must be some evidentiary basis before any public official is required to submit to a paternity test. And on this latter point, the burden is on the defendants here to show opportunity for intimate contact between the Deputy Mayor and Ms. Woodley which could have resulted in the conception of Ms. Woodley's son. Otherwise, any public figure, including dedicated public officials, such as the Deputy Mayor, would be subjected to the embarrassment of allegations of fathering bitches and bastards—oh, sorry, strike those words and use 'children out of wedlock' instead—by anyone walking in off the street. Allowing such behavior opens the door to extortion for many accused parties who may not take the principled stand my client is taking, and simply make the problem go away by the payment of money. Also, let us not be fooled or misled that there is such a thing as a confidential paternity test. Persons other than the parties and their attorneys will have to know that the Deputy Mayor is walking into some medical office to be tested for paternity. Even if the test is administered in a private place, such as his home, with only the person doing the test seeing the Deputy Mayor and the specimen identified as John Doe's specimen, word of the test can easily leak out and the Deputy Mayor's otherwise unblemished reputation ruined, even if the test is negative, as it surely will be. This is why any requirement for paternity testing must be premised on an evidentiary record that satisfies the court that there is substantial proof warranting the test."

JUDGE: "It appears that neither of you want to focus on the sealing and anonymous caption issues of the Order to Show Cause. So, I will rule on those on my own. And you both are fixated on the paternity test. So, I just may rule on that issue as well. Let's move toward wrapping this up. Mr. Forte, you have any rebuttal to Mr. Stillman?"

FORTE: "Yes, Your Honor. First of all, Mr. Stillman incorrectly assumes that the paternity test cannot be administered confidentially. This Court simply needs to issue an order ordering the facility doing the test to put its staff on notice that, besides the facility, that each staff person is subject to the order and the penalties that will flow from violating it. You can also assign a court referee to oversee the procedure to ensure the Deputy Mayor's confidentiality is respected every step of the way. Further, on the issue of confidentiality, once the paternity test is positive, the seal must be removed from this case's files, for then the public has the right to know whether the applicable law is applied the same for public officials as it is for a member of the general public."

STILLMAN: "Judge, let's cross that bridge when, and if, we ever get there."

JUDGE: "I agree. Go on, Mr. Forte."

FORTE: "Okay. Secondly, Deputy Mayor Gilbert cannot deny that he knows Ms. Woodley. For several years, she worked as night receptionist at the firm, which he founded and was the senior and managing partner. Nor can he deny that he was required by his firm's executive committee—and I will not embarrass him by stating the reason why—to take Ms. Woodley out to dinner. Also at that dinner was his longtime partner and colleague Joan Zakorski, who at some point was called away to handle some urgent client matter, leaving Ms. Woodley alone with the Deputy Mayor. It was toward the conclusion of that night, which rolled into the next day, where the opportunity for intimacy presented itself and happened. The following morning, Ms. Woodley found herself hung over, naked, and sharing the same bed with Deputy Mayor Gilbert. I suggest that the Deputy Mayor be put under oath and questioned about this. Should he deny it under oath, then let us proceed with an evidentiary hearing, the conclusion of which will not only require Gilbert to submit to a court-ordered paternity test but also subject him to a charge of perjury."

STILLMAN: "Judge, I most strenuously object to this absolute and complete outrage. You ordered me to apologize to Ms. Woodley moments ago. For what Mr. Forte just said, he deserves to be thrown back behind bars. Most fortunate for him this hearing is confidential, for I submit that if we were in open court his statements constitute plain and pure *de facto* defamation, and he would not be protected by the shield of immunity that protects attorneys for the statements they make while advocating for their clients."

JUDGE: "Okay, okay. I've heard enough. I will review the record and your pleadings and render my decision, which will likely happen within the coming week.

"In the interim, the dictates of the temporary restraining orders remain in full force and effect on both sides. I have already demonstrated my resolve to ensure that confidentiality be respected. I did not particularly enjoy having an attorney imprisoned, but I assure all of you, if I learn of another violation of the confidentiality order or any of the other aspects of the temporary restraining orders, the violating party will be jailed forthwith.

"Am I clear?"

Forte and Stillman in unison: "Yes."

JUDGE: "This hearing is now ended. Thank you, stenographer. You may pack up and take your leave."

The judge then asks us to stay awhile. He waits until the stenographer leaves and then addresses us:

"This is off the record, as I have dismissed the stenographer. I want you both to know that I have been in touch with the Commission on Judicial Conduct and apprised the Commission of the administrative judge's interference with my jurisdiction over this matter. So, I warn all of you, but especially you, Mr. Forte, and whoever communicated with the administrative judge on your behalf, that if there is any attempt to have the administrative judge run interference for any of you, it will be to no avail. The administrative judge will soon be apprised that he cannot stick his nose into what goes on in this courtroom. Now you are all dismissed. Good day."

Mary and I get up and leave the courtroom before Stillman and Gilbert.

Later I mention to Richie what Judge Joseph said about the administrative judge. Richie rolls his eyes and says, "That asshole Joseph is just trying to save face in front of you and the others. The Committee would ream him out if it were ever to investigate what he's bitchin' about and sees that he put you in jail without a shred of evidence."

CHAPTER 20

"The bitch set you up."

"AL, I GAVE you the home phone bill over a week ago to check the incoming calls. We need to make sure no one has tapped into our phone line and is making free calls."

"Okay, Theresa, I'll take a look."

It is beyond me why she is so concerned about this. Even if her bizarre suspicions are true, we are on a fixed-price plan and get billed the same amount each month regardless of phone calling volume.

But to make her happy, I glance over the bill and, lo and behold, notice on the list of incomings calls a call with a Chicago area code. Who called from Chicago?

Looking at the date and time of the call, I remember that the date was the day before my initial disaster of a meeting with Stillman and Gilbert at Joan's office. The time of the call is the same time that Peg Wells had called me. This isn't her cell phone number, but I now recall that she mentioned something about using a disposable phone.

That's right. She called to let me know that "they" knew we were talking and she was told that if she continued to talk to me, her chief clerkship appointment would be nixed.

That call upset me so much that I suppressed it, tucked it into the deepest recesses of my mind. I kept failing to remember it and more importantly failed to mention what I now finally recognize could be a significant detail.

An ominous feeling comes over me, and I realize that I had better find out from Mick the phone number of the phone used to make the call to the reporter. Prior to this point, there was no need for me to know it.

I call Mick. He tells me the number and it is the same phone number as the phone number for the phone that Peg used to call me.

"Mick, my friend Peggy Wells, who is now the chief clerk of Family Court, called me using a phone with that very same phone number the night before that midtown meeting with Stillman and Gilbert that you drove me to."

"Al, hold it a minute. You says her name's Peggy?"

"Yes. Why?"

"Ain't Peggy the nickname for Margaret?"

My stomach turns. "Yes, and I know for a fact that Margaret is Peggy's legal first name."

"Well, cuz, don't ya remember that Margaret is the name of Gilbert's *goomah*."

"Must be a coincidence, Mick."

"Well, let's see. Believe it or not, but JBJ takes his assignment seriously, and without our askin' him, he started to jot down phone numbers for the incomin' and outgoin' calls on Gilbert's cell phone."

"Shit! Why didn't we think to have him do that?"

"'Cause we ain't trusted him and didn't wanna give him too much to do. We kept his assignment to the simple shit. You know, like just lookin' for the Chicago phone number that made the call to the reporter. Simple stuff like that.

"So, Al, you know what this Peggy's or Margaret's cell phone number is?"

"Yeah."

"Okay, I'm gonna read you some of the numbers that were called to and from Gilbert's phone. Let me know if any are the same as hers."

The first phone number Mick reads to me is Peg's cell phone number.

"Well, Al, it so happens that yesterday Gilbert called that number four times and he received three calls from that number. The calls were as short as three minutes and as long as twenty minutes. And this is during workin' hours."

"No shit! I'll be a fucking son of a bitch.

"Wait! According to what JBJ heard the day before that conference in Philly, Gilbert went there not for the conference but 'to make some girl.' Peg must have been at the conference, and she or someone using the disposable phone she bought to call me also used it to call the reporter."

"Yeah. To call the reporter and land your ass in jail, don't forget.

"It's lookin' to me like, in the immortal words of Marion Barry, may he rest in peace, 'the bitch set you up,' cuz."

"Mick, this is much too much for me to take in. Peggy and I go way back and I have helped her so much over the years. I just can't believe she'd be involved in this way. I also can't believe that she'd let Gilbert seduce her."

"Well, looks like your real good friend done both. Who the fuck knows? That motherfucker Gilbert gotta have somethin' over her.

"This tells us why the phone number wasn't blocked from the reporter's caller ID. She ain't no pro, at least not that kinda pro."

"Mick, Peggy is no prostitute!"

"Forget that, but you remember the reporter Burke even says that the caller's voice sounded like some woman tryin' to sound like a man.

"Another thing. Max, the Amtrak guy, says that Gilbert was on that train that got to Philly after the time of the call to Burke. Not only did he find out that the ticket was scanned, but he even talked to the conductor who scanned it and the conductor remembered that Gilbert was one of the passengers on that train. You know, it sounded to me from what JBJ says that Gilbert was gonna 'make some girl,' but maybe he'd already done that and was just goin' there to shack up with her with the conference as a cover. Anyways, looks like he already had her unda his thumb, to keep the Stones rollin'."

"Fuck, fuck, fuck. What do we do about this?"

"We? No 'we,' but 'you,' cuz. You gotta talk to your so-called friend and see what she hasta say for herself."

"But how can I call her? She closed her office, gave up her practice, and could lose this position and the potential for judgeship if she's caught talking to me."

"Al, who the fuck you tryin' to help? Is it Mary or this obvious *putan*, who put you in jail and is now obviously strummin' that dick Gilbert's ole banjo?"

"I will have to figure something out."

"You can say that again. Just make sure you do it real quick. Time ain't exactly on our side, as I ain't gotta tell you."

As it turned out, the following morning the judge's decision was issued and he ruled that the defamation case's court file be sealed and permitted the plaintiff to be named anonymously. The decision and order also maintained in full force and effect the temporary restraining orders. Significantly, the decision and order retained jurisdiction of any paternity and child support proceeding, under the general jurisdiction vested in the Supreme Court, which supersedes the specific jurisdiction of the Family Court, and ordered that there be an evidentiary hearing in two weeks to determine whether there is sufficient evidence to order Gilbert to submit to a paternity test. The decision and order further provided that should a test be ordered and there is a finding of paternity, the matter would be transferred to the Family Court for a ruling on child support.

Two weeks were scant time to gather up the necessary evidence and witnesses. Mick and I agreed that my confrontation with Peggy would be put on hold for the time being so I could prioritize the preparation required for the critical evidentiary hearing. We also decided that it was better that Gilbert and Stillman not be aware that we know that Gilbert's *goomah* had made that call.

In the interim, Mick had The Olympiad staked out to see who went in and out with Gilbert. Working with a picture of Peggy from the *Law Journal*, which accompanied the article about her Family Court appointment, the person assigned to stake out the apartment building positively identified Peggy as Gilbert's frequent overnight visitor.

It wasn't easy, but I somehow managed to table my feelings of disappointment and betrayal so they would not mess with my concentration as I prepared for this absolutely critical juncture in Mary's case.

CHAPTER 21

"I threw a lamp at his fat head; unfortunately, I missed."

"Mick, I need Sammy or one of your other drivers to pick me up tomorrow at the garage in my parents' assisted living place. I need to get to that Starbucks in Glen Ridge again. Looks like we may have lucked out with the limo company. I'll know tomorrow."

Number one on my to-do list for the evidentiary hearing was Joan Zakorski, but she proved to be elusive. I called her office, and her secretary said, "Sorry, Mr. Forte, but I do not know where she is or when she will be back in the office." When I pressed for details, the secretary just repeated that she had no clue as to where Joan was or when she will be back in the office or even how to contact her.

When I called later and Joan's secretary gave me the same story, I was convinced that I was being given the runaround. I would later learn from Molly, when she finally returned my calls to her disposable phone, that Joan had just picked up and left for reasons not known to even the firm's senior management. The circumstances were a big mystery, as Joan was in the midst of preparing for a major transaction scheduled to close later in the week and the folks there were running around like chickens with their heads chopped off trying to get a partner to cover for Joan, as those assisting her were all junior associates.

Molly offered to assist me in any way she could. I told her I would get back to her if I thought of something.

I told Mick about this development and he followed up with both JBJ and Smitty and learned that, unsurprisingly, Gilbert was behind Joan's sudden disappearance. Smitty overheard Stillman yelling "Are you out of your mind!" to someone. Stillman's secretary told Smitty that Stillman was on the phone with "that crazy Deputy Mayor client."

Later that evening, JBJ reported to Mick that "some crazy lady" (based on JBJ's description, it was Joan) stormed into Gilbert's office and, even with the door closed, could be heard screaming at Gilbert, "You want me to leave town? Are you fuckin' nuts? I have a major deal closing in three days. It would take me a day to prepare another attorney to cover for me and you want me to leave tonight? You're out of your cockamamie mind!"

I still prepared a subpoena demanding that Joan appear at the evidentiary hearing and had duplicate originals served at her office and home. I eventually received a call from one of her law partners who informed me that no one at the firm knew where she went, how to reach her, or when she will return. He said he had the subpoena scanned and e-mailed to both her office and personal e-mail addresses, and got auto-replies from both accounts that Joan would not have e-mail access "indefinitely." Based on this, he advised me that it was unlikely that Joan would appear at the hearing.

Gilbert obviously coerced Joan to skip town. If she were available to testify she'd confirm that Gilbert and

Mary were alone on the night in question and that testimony would evidence contact and opportunity, and based on that the court would likely order Gilbert to submit to a paternity test. I considered forcing the issue, but decided to first see if there is another way to get evidence and witnesses that would eliminate the need for Joan's testimony.

Plan B consisted of contacting the different places where Mary and Gilbert were together on the night of the dinner. Those places consisted of the 21 Club, the several clubs that Mary remembered visiting with Gilbert, and The Olympiad, where Gilbert's pied-à-terre is located.

Both my and Mick's efforts to get any information out of any of those places proved fruitless.

We had little doubt that Gilbert or Stillman had contacted those establishments and instructed them not to cooperate. Nevertheless, Mick and I were also up against the existing privacy policies as well as the passage of time, as the night in question was a couple of years ago. Also, it was a single night, not an ongoing series of events over time. So, even if some record of guests or surveillance tapes were in play, chances were they were not stored or retained for very long. And this turned out to be pretty much true of all the places, except for The Olympiad.

The Olympiad did maintain and keep on file for a considerable period both guest sign-in sheets and surveillance tapes. However, the building had a very strict privacy policy, and while I could have subpoenaed its logs and tapes, I would not be able to get them in time for the evidentiary hearing, now less than two weeks away. Mick had some connections with the building services union.

Several of his men were union members and some even worked at The Olympiad from time to time to cover for the regular staff. However, none of Mick's contacts had any access to the information we needed. It would have been fabulous to see that Mary was signed in as Gilbert's guest sometime after midnight of the night of the dinner, or if there was a tape showing them making their way drunkenly through the lobby and into the elevator. Mick was able to identify the fellow who was at the front desk that morning, but when I spoke with Leonard Arnold, he could not recall ever seeing Mary (I showed him her picture) and denied ever seeing Gilbert go to his apartment with any woman other than his wife. When I asked Leonard to describe Gilbert's wife, he described Rosa Ortiz, the G&A office manager who had been Gilbert's mistress.

Then there was the limousine company and the limo driver. I did make inquiry of the car service firm that both Mary and I remembered G&A using at the time in question, but the manager informed me that they never had any limos as part of its fleet. Unfortunately, neither Mary nor I had a clue as to which company G&A used when it hired limousines for special occasions.

Fortunately, on her own initiative Molly mulled over how she would proceed with Joan's absence, and she wondered where else she would look for evidence. She doubted investigating the various establishments visited by Mary and Gilbert would yield anything, which we already had found out. But Molly thought maybe the limo driver kept his own ride log and maybe we could track him down. Molly happened to know that G&A's office manager Rosa

Ortiz made all limo arrangements, and more importantly, Molly knew how to reach Rosa and coordinated a meeting for us at that Starbucks in Glen Ridge.

Both Rosa and Molly were at Starbucks by the time NJ Transit got me there.

Rosa had never looked so relaxed and radiant. She shared with us that she was young and foolish when she started working at the firm and that Gilbert paid attention to her right away. She kept getting promoted and, before she knew it, she was Gilbert's personal secretary, which is when the affair started. She was attracted to his brilliance and confidence, and at first thought that the bullying was what made him such a powerful and respected lawyer. She was blinded to its effects on other people.

Gilbert fathered a son with her, and, though he never legally acknowledged the child as his, Rosa said he did support them by giving her salary raises far in excess of those given to other G&A staff, including associates. With Gilbert's power, no one questioned Rosa's substantial salary raises, though before the mergers that increased the firm's size significantly, it was unlikely that anyone was even aware of them. By the time other partners saw what Rosa was being paid, she had risen to the position of office manager and was such a top-notch administrator with highly touted abilities, the firm's senior partners felt she was worth every penny she was paid.

As the firm grew, how it conducted itself had to go up a level or two so it was commensurate with its stature among other law firms. This meant, among other things, that when it entertained special guests, whether prospective clients or highly regarded existing ones, the meals had to be more lavish and the restaurants the best of the best, with no expense spared. It also meant that the transportation for these meals needed to be upgraded, and the senior partners asked Rosa to line up a suitable limousine company to provide the necessary transport.

It so happened that Rosa's cousin, Jose Aponte, had a newly established limousine company and he and his partners were owner-drivers. To help her cousin get off the ground, she gave Jose's firm G&A's business, with the warning that that business relationship would end if it did not live up to the highest expectations of G&A's partners and of the clients being entertained.

Rosa admitted that an ulterior motive in retaining Jose's firm was her desire to have someone report back to her about Gilbert's behavior while he was entertaining firm guests, particularly female guests. She watched Gilbert becoming more and more flirtatious and suspected that despite their more than a dozen years together, he was unfaithful to her.

Besides her suspicions about his womanizing, she also become increasingly troubled by the way he treated certain people. She was aware of how spiteful he was toward clients who chose to leave the firm and she was very much aware of, and appalled by, the malicious deeds perpetrated by Gilbert on patent attorney Robert Herman. Without sharing any particulars, she admitted to hating herself for not doing anything to help "that poor, poor man."

So, when she heard of Mary's predicament from Molly, she was ready—and most willing—to help in any way she could.

"Al, first, the Executive Committee not only insisted that Gilbert take Mary out for a really nice dinner to compensate for the terrible way he treated her, but the chairperson in particular insisted that I join Gilbert that evening. I was ready to go, but most unfortunately for Mary, I was not able to. My son was rushed to the hospital that afternoon with an appendicitis attack and we had to twist Joan's arm to get her to go in my place at the last minute.

"Anyway, right after that night, Jose reported to me about Gilbert's behavior going to all these clubs after the restaurant and about Mary being really drunk, and probably stoned, and Gilbert groping her in the limo. He also reported that when he dropped them at The Olympiad, he helped the doorman virtually drag Mary into the building, and then Gilbert's dismissed him at around four that morning.

"Gilbert was, and still is, such a fucking pig. Let me hold my tongue!

"Anyway, I spoke to Jose yesterday and he not only remembers that night vividly, but he also kept a record of what happened. Jose will be available to assist you in any way. I made sure of that."

"Wow! Thanks, Rosa. This is a tremendous help.

"But how are you doing, Rosa, since G&A broke up."

"In a way, that was the best thing that could have happened to me. It forced me to honestly review my relationship with that prick Gilbert, and I realized it was time for me to move on. When I informed that bastard of this, his response was, 'Yeah, I guess it's best for me to move on as well.' I threw a lamp at his fat head; unfortunately, I missed.

"Luckily for me, by that point our son was in high school, and I had saved enough money so I no longer needed Gilbert's support. I was luckier still because I found a real, genuinely nice man with whom I have found true love and whom I plan to marry next month, so I have no worries about my son or me or our future."

"That's wonderful, Rosa.

"Well, thank you both for your tremendous help. I will contact Jose to go over his testimony and to coordinate his arrival in court. We'll have him stay in one of my cousin's places the night before, so we can eliminate the possibility of dirty tricks on Gilbert's part."

"Yes, Al. You certainly need to be prepared for whatever outrage that prick has up his sleeve."

"He already worked it so I had to spend a weekend in jail."

"That no good, motherfucking son of a bitch. Sorry Molly and Al, but he is such a terrible person."

"You're preaching to the choir, Rosa."

"If there is any other way whatsoever I can help, don't hesitate to call me. We must bring that bastard down once and for all! And give my number to your cousin and the rest of your team in case they need to reach me when you're not available. Consider me a member of your team."

CHAPTER 22

"Mary's been Herman'd."

"MR. APONTE, YOU testified that you dropped off Mr. Gilbert and Ms. Woodley at The Olympiad at approximately 3:30 a.m. that particular morning, is that correct?"

"Yes, sir, Mr. Forte. During that job, like for all my jobs even to today, in fact, I keep a sheet where I make note of all the places that I take the passengers, as well as the time of arrival at and departure from each place. I also write down anything I think is noteworthy."

"And, just to confirm, what you handed me earlier, and which the judge labeled Exhibit A, is a true and complete copy of the sheet you maintained for the night and morning of the job where you first picked up Ms. Woodley from her home in the East Village, from where you drove her to the 21 Club, then drove her and Mr. Gilbert to the several clubs noted, and then finally to The Olympiad. Is that correct?"

"Yes, Mr. Forte, that is a complete and exact copy of my notes for that job."

"Among your so-called noteworthy comments, you wrote that they both appeared to be, and I quote, 'tipsy' when they left the 21 Club."

"Yes."

"Okay, let me continue, and then as the night then morning progressed, they got more and more drunk and then even high. Correct?"

"Yes, Mr. Forte. I did not put this in my sheets, but they did smoke some grass while in my car."

"Mr. Aponte, why did you not note this on your job sheet?"

"To be honest, Mr. Forte, I didn't think it wise to make note of that kind of information. It is illegal to possess marijuana and I didn't want to create problems for my customers, especially make trouble for Rosa's boss."

"But you also noted that they were hugging and kissing and Mr. Gilbert was groping Ms. Woodley?"

"Yes. There is nothing illegal about that. Ms. Woodley seemed to be going along with it, although once we arrived at The Olympiad, she appeared to be quite out of it and the doorman and I had to carry her into the building."

"Did you assist Ms. Woodley through the lobby into the elevator and up to an apartment?"

"No. Once we got into the lobby, Mr. Gilbert said that he and the doorman would manage from there and that my services were no longer needed."

"Okay. What time was that and did you make note of the doorman's name?"

"It was just about 3:40 a.m., Mr. Forte, and I recall that the doorman's name was Leonard Arnold. I wrote it on the sheet."

"How do you know his name? Did he introduce himself?"

"No. I read it off the name tag on his uniform. Also, Mr. Gilbert addressed him as Lenny."

"Okay. That concludes the questions I have for you, Mr. Aponte."

Judge Joseph then asks Stillman if he liked to question the witness. Stillman turns his head and whispers to Gilbert. Gilbert, with his eyes bugging out some, mouths an empathic "no" to Stillman, who informs the judge he had no questions for the witness. I am a bit perplexed that Gilbert didn't want Stillman to at least torture Aponte some, have him at least squirm a little for the problem he just created for Gilbert.

The judge then thanks Aponte for coming and informs him that he's dismissed. I whisper my thanks to him and Jose gets up and leaves.

Just after Jose exits, there is a knock on the door of the closed courtroom, where now it's just me, Stillman, Gilbert, a court officer, the court stenographer, the judge's law secretary, and the judge. The judge instructs the officer to see who's there and to bring Mary in as she is next up to testify and should be waiting her turn in the hallway. (I am concerned about Mary, for she had not arrived by 9:30 a.m., the time I instructed her to be at the courtroom, even though she would be sitting outside during Jose's testimony. I calm myself with the thought that Mick's driver probably got stuck in traffic and she arrived late and will be walking in right then.)

The officer goes to the door and comes back without Mary but accompanied by another court officer. The officer whispers something to the judge and then leaves.

The judge, with a puzzled look on his face, then addresses us, "The chief court officer sent Officer Thompson to report that Ms. Woodley was arrested at the courthouse checkpoint as she sought admittance to the court house this morning. Apparently, some container with a substance thought to be cocaine was found on her."

I jump up, look wild-eyed in Gilbert's direction and scream, "You rotten bastard! You set her up!"

The judge bangs his gavel, stands up and shouts, "Order in this court! Mr. Forte, get control of yourself. No one uses such language in my court! You are out of order!"

Stillman takes his turn and jumps up and says, "Judge, this is an absolute disgrace and warrants sanctions!"

The judge replies, "Yes, Mr. Forte's outburst is disgraceful. He had better comport himself or he will be held in contempt. In fact, were this not a closed hearing, he would be on his way back to jail this very moment. However, this being a closed session and given that his outburst was in reaction to a surely unsettling shock, I will give him some time to get his emotions in check. And, unless he has a yearning for jailhouse cuisine, I am confident he will conduct himself as a professional for the rest of this session."

I am so pissed and upset and ready to let loose again when there is another knock on the door. Exasperated now, the judge looks at the officer and tells her to see who is disturbing us now, and the officer goes to the door, speaks with someone and turns toward the judge and announces it is some attorney who says he needs to talk to me right away.

The judge sighs and says to me, "Okay, go and see what that attorney wants. And in fact, let's recess for ten minutes. Use the time to calm yourself down, Mr. Forte. But be back here in ten minutes."

Richie Abbatello is waiting for me in the hall.

I say to him, "Mary's been arrested!"

He responds, "Al, come with me quick to the men's room. There are things we need to discuss in private."

We rush down the hall to the men's room.

Richie says, "Mary's been Herman'd."

"So I heard!

"Look, Rich, one of Mick's guys was supposed to get her here this morning. How the fuck can they Herman her with all the precautions we took?"

"Al, listen to me. When she went through security downstairs, they found what they suspect is coke in her pocket. Mick called me right away and I am waiting for the arraignment so she can get bailed out."

I shout, "That no-good, motherfucking, cocksucking son of a bitch! I'm gonna go in there and kick that scumbag right in the balls!"

Richie slaps my face.

"Hey, what's that for?"

"Mick said I'd need to do that. He says you must maintain your composure. We will get this situation under control. Get a grip and go in there and conduct yourself like the pro you are."

"What the fuck are you talking about? How could I possibly not react angrily to this bullshit?"

"You are going to do it for the good of your client. Hear me?"

All sorts of craziness are running through my brain, but somehow my anger does begin to subside. Slowly, the lawyerly front reemerges.

"Okay. I'll calm down and go in there like a lawyer with my emotions in check. But at some point, Gilbert is going to get his."

"Al, Mick is on it. He won't allow Gilbert to get away with shit. Just keep that in mind in case your Neapolitan blood starts to boil again and get the better of you. Mick says he will meet up with you at your office when you're finished here. In the meanwhile, I'm working to get Mary released on bail."

I return to the courtroom. I am much calmer now.

The judge continues, "Okay, Mr. Forte, I trust this little respite steadied your nerves and we can continue in a constructive fashion. Right off, let me say that I must consider what effect, if any, Ms. Woodley's arrest has over the matter at this juncture."

Composed now, I say, "Your Honor, Mary hasn't been convicted of anything. And even if she eventually is, that has no bearing whatsoever on whether we have provided the requisite evidence—and I am confident that Mr. Aponte's uncontroverted testimony does that—to establish that the Deputy Mayor and my client had the opportunity to become intimate and together conceive baby Roger."

The judge responds, "I do not know if you're correct and I must do some thinking before I issue my order."

Gilbert whispers something to Stillman and he stands up and says, "Judge, Ms. Woodley's arrest is germane to whether she is fit to be a mother. Of course, that would be an issue upon her conviction on the drug charge. It certainly would impact any child support proceeding, for if she should be ruled to be an unfit mother and the child is taken from her, then any support would not be paid to her but to whomever is raising the child, whether a family member or a foster parent, or whomever."

I say, working hard to stay calm, "Your Honor, Mr. Stillman has the cart two miles in front of its horse. This speculation just causes confusion. Let's just take this one step at a time.

"Your Honor, please proceed with your ruling regarding a paternity test based on this hearing and then we will take it from there."

Stillman gets up again and says, "We object, Judge. You may want to hold off on any ruling until more is known of Ms. Woodley's arrest. As I already indicated, it will have a direct impact on support proceedings."

I stand up again and say as calmly as I can, "Again, the issue at this moment is paternity. And even in the unlikely event Mary is ultimately deemed incapable of properly raising her son, whoever is found to be the father will have the obligation to support Roger, whether raised by his mother or someone else."

Judge Joseph throws up his hands and exclaims, "Enough. I will take this all under advisement, but I must say that Mr. Forte's last point is well taken. In any event, I will issue my ruling shortly. And if I rule that Deputy Mayor Gilbert must submit to a paternity test, the testing process will be overseen by a referee to ensure that confidential controls are in place and followed to the letter.

"This hearing is concluded. Good day, all."

I rush out of the courtroom. I had to catch up with Mick to find out what the hell is going on.

CHAPTER 23

"You gotta trust me."

"MICK, I HAVE to know how, after all of the planning we did, with the informants we have in place, with all we've done to make sure any dirty tricks are thwarted, how the fuck could they possibly manage to do to Mary what they did to Herman?

"It wasn't even something new. An exact rerun of Herman, of which we were fully aware. What the fuck happened?"

Mick says, "Al, don't get yourself all excited. Things are unda control. Mary's bailed out and she's back in her apartment restin'."

"Yeah, but what the fuck's going to happen if she gets convicted? She and Roger are fucked! I can't believe we let this happen. And when I say 'we' I really mean me because, as I've said all along, whatever goes wrong is my sole responsibility."

Mick replies, "Listen Al, this here's kinda funny. I'm the one who usually gets all excited and wants to kill someone. Now, I gotta calm you down and get you to take a chill pill."

Just then, Francesca comes into my office and tells me that Stillman and Gilbert are on the phone and they say it's urgent that we talk. I tell her to have them hold.

Mick says, "Close your door and talk to 'em with the speaker on. I need to hear what they say. If I gotta tell you something, I'll hit the mute button and tell you. Okay?"

Exasperated, and totally unsure about what to do, I say, "Okay."

I hit the speaker button on my phone.

"Hello, Mr. Stillman? I understand both you and your client are on the phone."

"That is correct, Mr. Forte."

"Among other things, we want to let you know how terrible we feel about what transpired with your client this morning. We may be adversaries, but we are also human beings and our hearts go out to your client."

"I'm sure your hearts do," I say in a manner tinged with sarcasm.

Mick hit the mute button and with eye bulging says, "Listen to what they say. Don't react like that. Don't get pissed no matter what!"

With the phone still muted, I ask, "Why?"

Mick responds, "Just fuckin' do it! You gotta trust me. Just listen!"

I decide at that instant, despite not understanding why at all, that I'll do as Mick directs.

Stillman's reply, spoken while the phone is muted, is, "I detect sarcasm in your voice. Please take us seriously. Our concern for your client is sincere. We have no doubt that the stress of being a single mother and this litigation surely contributed to her turning to narcotics for comfort. Nevertheless, our position remains that she had deluded herself that the deputy mayor had fathered her child. It's tragic that her intoxicated state that night wiped out any memory of what really occurred."

I roll my eyes till they almost fly off my face.

"Well, I will convey your sincere concerns to my client."

Mick nods and I almost gag.

Stillman continues, "Thank you, sir. Now, besides sending our sincerest best wishes, we also felt it important to make a proposal that would bring closure to this episode in a manner that works in the best interest for all sides, especially that poor child."

I say, "I am all ears."

Mick nods and gives me the okay sign.

"This proposal will require that your client make a painfully honest assessment of her addiction. I know you and she do not agree, but if the deputy mayor is required to submit to a paternity test, it will be negative. The ultimate ramification of this finding will be that this poor child will end up in foster care, for at the end of the day Ms. Woodley will be ruled unfit due to her addiction. And even if such a ruling is not forthcoming, she will not be in any position to adequately support her child for there will be no other means of support, other than social services.

"What we propose will require that Ms. Woodley make a difficult choice, but whichever choice she makes is better than the reality I just described. Please listen attentively without interrupting and then carefully consider the following with your client, once she is released from custody, as I assume Mr. Abbatello will get her bailed out soon."

Mick nods to me and I say, "That's right."

"We propose two options for Ms. Woodley to consider. Her first option is to release Deputy Mayor Gilbert from any claims she has with respect to paternity and child support. This release will yield her a payment of $100,000 to assist her to sort out her affairs with the child. It will give her a nest egg in case she is permitted to retain custody of Roger and it will also permit her to pursue a paternity and child support action against the appropriate party, her former boyfriend. We are aware that there was an alleged negative paternity test, but we very much doubt that test's validity.

"Alternatively, and this is the second option, Deputy Mayor Gilbert is willing to admit paternity without the need for any test. He will accept full custody of the child and Ms. Woodley will surrender her parental rights. A $100,000 payment will also accompany this option. This way Ms. Woodley can fully devote her time to getting proper drug treatment, which would be more feasible if she had no child care responsibilities."

After Stillman finishes with his bullshit, Mick mutes the phone and says, "Doncha react. Listen to me! Tell 'em you'll get back to 'em tomorrow. Tell 'em they gotta be in *your* office tomorrow so you can let 'em know your client's decision."

Somehow, my head does not explode and I say, "Gentlemen, I will need to mull this over and discuss it with my client, her criminal defense attorney, and the social worker. I do intend to fast track this. Let's meet in my office tomorrow at three. By then, I should know if she is willing to accept either of those options, and we can preliminarily memorialize it pending the drafting of the formal settlement documents."

Stillman responds, "We'd prefer to meet at my office, but we will accommodate your request, especially since you have a lot to do in anticipation of that meeting and you would not want to waste time traveling to midtown."

"Fine. Thanks. You know where my office is. I will see you both here tomorrow. It is my hope that we wrap this up at that time."

After I hang up the phone, I stare at Mick. He says, "Listen. You done good. I gotta get outa here and take care of somethings quick. Tonight, be at my office at 7:30. You, me, and Richie have lots to go over."

CHAPTER 24

"We have you by the short hairs."

STILLMAN AND GILBERT'S limo pulls up in front of my office moments before three the following day. As they enter, Francesca greets them at the door and escorts them past two nicely dressed but rather large men, one black and the other Latino, sitting patiently in the waiting area, into the conference room where I'm sitting.

Francesca tells me later she heard Gilbert snicker to Stillman derogatorily about the "high class" of clients I service.

Francesca offers them coffee and tea and some nice Italian pastry from a local bakery. Francesca serves everyone, closes the conference room door behind her, and then returns to her desk.

After some pleasantries about Italian pastries and about the history of this traditional working-class Italian neighborhood that's becoming increasingly gentrified, we get down to business.

"Well, after much discussion back and forth, my client did make a decision."

Stillman says, "Well, I must say that this is most gratifying and, honestly, surprising, news."

Just then the conference room door opens and in strides Mick, followed by my prison roommate Vernon

Daniels and Paolo Ruiz, one of Pedro Ramos's guys, who are the men who were sitting in the waiting room. Vernon and Paolo stand in front of the conference room door with their arms folded, obviously intending to block anyone's exit.

Gilbert looks at Mick and the others with utter disdain and says, "Who the fuck are you and your friends?"

"We're your worst nightmare, asshole! I'm Al's cousin and these here are a coupla friends of mine."

"John, let's get the fuck out of here."

Mick says, "Youse ain't goin' nowheres 'til I says so."

Gilbert replies, "Listen you fat Guinea, who the fuck you think you're talking to? I'm the First Deputy Mayor of this city. I will have the police swarming all over your ass after we're finished here."

Mick says, "Let me have the honor to tell youse Mary's response to your offer. She says there ain't no fuckin' way she could accept your bullshit offer, and she wants both of youse to take it and shove it right up your big, fat asses!"

Gilbert stands up and screams, "This is fucked up. You have us come all the way to Dagoville to listen to this dreck? What the fuck gives you the right to disrespect us this way?"

Mick says, "Look who's the fuck's talkin' about respect? Number one, we ain't appreciated your arrangin' for that phone call to that reporter that landed my cousin in jail."

Gilbert cuts in, "You don't have a clue about what the fuck you are talking about. I had nothing whatsoever to do with that call. I was heading to Philly on Amtrak and was somewhere between Metro Park and Trenton at the time my attorney says the call was made."

Gilbert smirks and continues, "But to tell you the truth, I kicked myself for not making that brilliant move myself. It was pure genius, but I regret—and am frankly embarrassed to admit—that I deserve no credit for it."

Gilbert was so adamant that I found him believable. Given the immediate commotion at hand, I filed this away for future consideration.

Stillman pulls Gilbert back into his chair and says to me, "Mr. Forte, I am shocked and outraged. Have you lost all sense of propriety?

"We must take our leave."

Mick says, "Youse ain't goin' nowheres til law enforcement gets here."

Gilbert says, "What the fuck are you talking about, law enforcement? I already told you I am the First Deputy Mayor."

Mick replies, "Shut the fuck up, you piece of shit."

Right then, there is a knock on the door and Richie Abbatello walks in accompanied by several men in suits and a couple of uniformed police officers.

One of the suits speaks, "Good day, gentlemen. I am Special Agent Adams with the Federal Bureau of Investigation."

Gilbert seems confused and asks, "What are you doing here and what do the feds have to do with any of this?"

Agent Adams continues, "Good afternoon, Deputy Mayor Gilbert, and you must be his attorney, John Stillman. We are here to arrest you, Mr. Gilbert, for possession of cocaine and for the other crimes that are set forth in this arrest warrant that I am handing your attorney."

Stillman stands up and says, "Sir, this is entirely uncalled for. You are claiming that the deputy mayor possesses cocaine and committed the crimes listed here? This is utter nonsense."

Adams continues, "Sir, within the last several hours we executed a search warrant, which allowed a search of Mr. Gilbert's apartment in The Olympiad. We discovered there several thousand grams of cocaine in its purest form. We compared what we found in the apartment with the powder that our agents witnessed being placed into Ms. Woodley's pocket yesterday morning by Court Officer Thompson, and they match. We even compared those stashes with what was found on the person of Robert Herman, whom I understand Mr. Gilbert knows, and they match as well.

"My associate will now read Deputy Mayor Gilbert his Miranda rights."

Gilbert stands and shouts, "Go shove Miranda up your ass!"

Stillman gives Gilbert a stern look and says, "Gordon, I must advise you to remain silent."

Gilbert responds with, "Screw you! No one tells me what to do!"

Stillman now stands and yells, "God damn you, Gordon, for once in your life shut the fuck up!"

After a moment, the raised eyebrows are lowered, things quiet down, and the Miranda warning is read.

Stillman says, "My criminal defense partner will be taking over the representation of Mr. Gilbert. She will be in touch with the assigned U.S. Attorney."

Adams continues, "Fine. And by the way, you may or may not recall this gentleman here. He is John Zachs, the attorney who assisted in the ultimate exoneration of Robert Herman. While Mr. Herman's conviction for possession of cocaine was overturned on appeal and his disbarment vacated, the personal setbacks resulting from his arrest continue to wreak havoc on his life. We have strong reasons to believe that Mr. Herman's arrest was orchestrated by Mr. Gilbert. We are uncertain what action if any can now be brought against Mr. Gilbert for what we believe he did to Mr. Herman, but we will try. Nevertheless, we have you, Mr. Gilbert, by the short hairs with respect to Ms. Woodley."

Richie then steps up and adds, "And, Mr. Stillman and Mr. Gilbert, Mary was released without being charged, because we knew about Mr. Gilbert's plan to subvert justice, and Gilbert and his accomplice, Court Officer Thompson, played right into our hands. Thompson's been taken into custody and confessed about his and Gilbert's role in Mary's false arrest. Both he and Gilbert will be doing time. By the way, the feds will be happy to permit Gilbert to undergo a paternity test. Judge Joseph's ruling just came down and it orders that Gilbert be tested. Also, the judge was informed that Thompson was arrested and that Gilbert's arrest was pending and indicated that upon confirmation of both, he will lift the seal from the defamation case's file."

As Gilbert is led out of my conference room in handcuffs with what is probably an unprecedented doomed look on his face, Mick says to him, "My cousin sure is some candy-ass pansy, ain't he?"

Gilbert just keeps walking wearily out the door and into the waiting police car.

CHAPTER 25

"How it all worked out."

"**I want to** know why you fuckers kept me in the dark about what was going on. First, you, Rich, in that bathroom, you even slap me. Mary gets 'Herman'd' and I must keep my cool with no explanation whatsoever about everything that's happening behind my back?

"I was supposed to control this matter, be in command, be kept in the loop, but at the most critical time, the very moment of truth, I'm deliberately left in the dark. I'm pissed!"

Richie says, "Sorry, Al, but at that moment things were happening real fast and furious and there just wasn't time to fill you in. In fact, things hadn't fully played out yet and it would have been premature to tell you anything."

"You don't know what stress it caused me. And then you, Mick, you who said that you'd keep me apprised about what you're up to. You're keeping secrets from me, which I hope you'll now tell me about so, at a minimum, I know whether my license is at risk. I got such a headache.

"And Mary tells me you gave her prior warning to go with whatever happens at the courthouse, to stay cool, don't panic, everything is under control. You didn't want to stress her out. Me, I'm so friggin' stressed, so shaken, I'm on the verge of a fuckin' stroke!"

Mick says, "Al, calm your ass down. We got things unda control. We figured out the shit they were up to and hadda bust our humps to pull everything together, Herman's attorney, the FBI, the NYPD, the chief court officer. Ain't had the time to tell you. Besides you got enough on your mind with that hearing. When Richie and me had a second to breathe, we were gonna call you and fill you in, but then we says it's better to tell you nuttin' til now, after the hearing. You're a shit actor, so if you knew all that was goin' good and Gilbert was done for, you'd've been relieved. But you really needed to be a nervous wreck. Listen, we did it for Mary's best interest and it's workin' out and you ain't in no hospital.

"Like I says things are unda control. The last pieces are gonna be played out tomorrow and you're gonna be happy with everythin'."

This was that 7:30 meeting that Mick ordered me to be at, after I ate shit first in court and then on the phone with Gilbert and Stillman when they made that fucked-up offer for poor, supposedly drugged-up, Mary.

In truth, Mick and Richie had no real choice but to handle what was happening the way they did. There was little time to keep me in the loop, even if I wasn't otherwise consumed with final preparation for the evidentiary hearing and then at the actual hearing, while the drama in the courthouse security checkpoint was being played out.

In retrospect, I must acknowledge Mick's genius for lining up informants at Stillman's and Gilbert's offices. I had every confidence in Smitty, particularly given his military background. But I had grave doubts and very deep concerns about JBJ, whom I considered a whacko not worthy of much trust. Thankfully, I was very wrong about that guy.

How it all worked out was a thing of beauty.

Two days before the evidentiary hearing, Smitty reported to Mick that he overheard Stillman shouting, "I do not know why you're calling me. I don't like one bit what you're saying and it is both improper and illegal." Smitty found out from Stillman's secretary that she had just put through a call to Stillman from a court officer named Thompson.

That night, JBJ told Mick that a court officer named Thompson had stopped by to see Gilbert. JBJ knew he was a court officer because he was in uniform and got his name from his name tag. Gilbert had JBJ close the door once he asked Thompson to come in but JBJ overheard Thompson yelling, "Is that all I'm gonna get? That ain't enough!" Thompson left the office in a huff, according to JBJ.

These reports got Mick thinking. Not wanting to disturb me, he knew I was stressed enough about the upcoming evidentiary hearing, he called Richie to report what he heard from Smitty and JBJ. Mick wanted Rich's take on Thompson.

Richie said that he needed to reach Johnny Zachs, Herman's attorney, to see if Thompson had any connection with what had happened to Robert Herman.

A half hour later, Richie told Mick that Thompson was the court officer who wanded and then arrested Herman. He said Zachs had gotten his brother, an FBI special agent, to have the Bureau look into what had happened to

Herman. The FBI did investigate, but despite suspecting that Herman was set up by Gilbert with the assistance of Thompson, it put its investigation on hold because there was no solid evidence to justify committing the resources necessary to continue it. Richie also said that Zachs reported that the chief of the court officers, named Nelson, also suspected Thompson of having a role in setting Herman up.

Richie reported that Zachs agreed to call his brother and pass on this current information about Thompson and Gilbert, and about Mary having to be at the evidentiary hearing in two days. Zachs thought the FBI may just want to pick up where they left off regarding Herman.

Zachs also mentioned that the FBI was also very interested in the cocaine that was found on Herman. It was pure and not the quality that one would ordinarily find on the street. He said that any leads about the source of the cocaine would go a long way toward further enticing the FBI to jump on what was happening now between Mary and Gilbert. The FBI had held onto the stash that was found in Herman's pocket.

Mick then said, "Rosa."

Richie asked, "Rosa? Who's she?"

"She used to be Gilbert's *goomah* during his big shot law firm days. Al saw her about the limousine company but I don't think they talked about much else, 'cept she told Al to call her if she could help. It's gettin' a little late, but fuck it, let's call her. You stay on, I finally figured out how this conferencin' thing works on this friggin' phone."

Mick and Richie called Rosa, but knowing Gilbert as she did, she first asked Mick to prove to her he is Al's cousin by telling her the name of Al's childhood pet.

Mick said, "Sure, Cindy, a beautiful French poodle."

"Okay, you pass the test. Only someone close to Al would know that. Nice to meet you, and Rich. Like I told Al, I want to help any way I can. I feel so much guilt for not doing more for that poor man, Robert Herman."

Mick asked if she ever heard of Court Officer Thompson. She hadn't. Then he asked if she knew anything about the cocaine that was found on Herman.

"Shamefully, I have to admit I do know about the cocaine. I would stay a night or two each week at Gilbert's apartment at The Olympiad. One night, I opened a drawer in a dresser that I used and the drawer came out of its compartment. I noticed it looked too short, like it had been altered. I then saw there was a little compartment behind where the rest of the drawer should be. In that compartment, I found an envelope that contained a number of plastic bags containing white powder. I put everything back the way it was and never said anything about it to Gilbert.

"I did later question him about what I heard happened to Herman, that he went to jail, got disbarred, and that that the experience had ruined him-but Gilbert denied having anything to do with it. But I know the way his face would blush when he lied, and he blushed that way when he made this denial. I wish I had had the guts to do something then."

Richie asked, "Do you know where the cocaine came from?"

"I suspect it came from a Colombian client of G&A. I would translate some of the conversations, and there was one call that was very peculiar. The client's principal, someone named Sanchez, was in the States and had come to our office. I was out that day, but I was told that Sanchez brought his own translator. I suspect they had devised some kind of code, because on a subsequent call Sanchez was talking about a special package and about some roundabout manner of payment for the package involving an offshore bank in the Bahamas. I couldn't quite decipher what they were talking about, but Gilbert told me to translate the exact words and leave the rest to him."

Richie asked, "You have any reason to know if the envelope with those packets would still be in that compartment?"

"Assuming he hasn't given them away or sold them, I doubt he would move it. I never let on that I discovered them."

"Rosa, this is a big help. We'll let you know if we have any further questions and we'll let you know what happens."

"Please do."

Mick and Richie both concluded that Mary or I would be Herman'd. After some debate, they figured it was more likely Mary, as it was she who had to be done in, in order to eliminate the threat to Gilbert.

Then, Mick remembered that JBJ's duties included his picking up dry cleaning from a dry cleaner near The Olympiad and to bring it up to Gilbert's apartment. The doorman would give him the key.

"Let me call JBJ now and tell him to go there tomorrow and to check and see if that envelope is still in that compartment. I'll get him gloves to wear, so he don't leave no prints behind. If he confirms the shit's still there, you get the FBI to get a search warrant based on Rosa's testimony—I gotta keep JBJ outa this part—that she seen what looked like cocaine in that spot. This way the FBI don't have to waste time there. I will arrange that a building service union guy I know is the doorman when the feds do the search, so word ain't gonna get back to Gilbert.

"You gotta call Zachs. The FBI gotta have undercover guys at the courthouse security checkpoint for when Mary goes through. I betcha that this guy Thompson is gonna slip a metal container with coke into her coat pocket without her knowin' it just before he waves the wand over her. We need the undercover feds to look out for this and, if possible, get pictures of it. If it goes down like that, Mary is gonna be taken into custody, but then we gotta get Chief Court Officer Nelson to release her, since she ain't done shit. And they can't do anything with Thompson 'til they've searched Gilbert's apartment and compare the coke found there with the coke that was on Mary and on Herman.

"After Nelson takes Mary into custody, he gotta release her to one of my guys in the courthouse garage. We need to work this all out with him right away so my guy has his okay to be in that garage. It all gotta happen without Thompson knowin' nuttin' about it.

"Now, Rich, you think it's gonna be a problem that Mary's ain't at that hearing?

"No, probably not. Jose's testimony should be enough."

"Okay. I'm gonna need you to be in court tomorrow. You gotta let Al know that Mary's been arrested. That the same shit they pulled on Herman, they done to her. But that's all you tell him. You gotta tell him not to get pissed, to keep his cool. Just tell him to trust us and that everything gonna work out at the end. You got that?"

"I hear you, Mick. Now, how is it gonna play out with Gilbert?"

"I'm gamblin' that once Mary's arrested, Gilbert and Stillman will move real quick to get Al and Mary to fall into some trap they gonna set for 'em. I betcha they're gonna have some offer they think Mary ain't could refuse. I'll be in Al's office with him when he's back from the hearing, and make sure he says the right thing. I'm gonna tell him to tell 'em they'll get Mary's answer the followin' day and they're gonna hafta come to Al's office to wrap things up.

"After this call, get Rosa on the phone and tell her the FBI will need her to testify or sign some affidavit or whatever, so that a judge will give 'em a search warrant and—I assume JBJ'll find what I pray to God he'll find—they go there, find the coke and then come to Al's office and put Gilbert's ass in the slammer."

Richie says, "Wow, Mick. Looks like you pretty much got this all figured out."

"Well somebody gotta do some thinkin' around here. My cousin's a good lawyer but he's a nervous wreck. And he thought he ain't needed my help!"

As it turned out, Mick did have it all figured out and it sure did play out just as he said it would.

CHAPTER 26

"Passed with flying colors."

As Richie reported when Gilbert was arrested, Judge Joseph ruled that I provided sufficient evidence to show the opportunity of intimacy between Gilbert and Mary, warranting Gilbert's being required to submit to a paternity test.

The judge would take judicial notice of Gilbert's arrest for not only possession of cocaine, but also for attempting to interfere with the administration of justice by conspiring with Court Officer Thompson to place a canister of cocaine in Mary's pocket. Having received from NYPD and the FBI formal notification of Gilbert's arrest and the charges against him, Judge Joseph, on his own initiative, ordered that the file for the defamation case no longer be sealed and kept from the public, that Gilbert be the named plaintiff, and that the restraints of the temporary restraining orders be vacated, which eliminated the confidentiality requirement and the prohibition on Mary's bringing a paternity and child support action.

I promptly did commence that action, to bring Mary's paternity and child support claims against Gilbert within the jurisdiction of the Family Court.

Gilbert's criminal prosecution was a federal case because of Gilbert's position as a public official and because the cocaine in Gilbert's possession was from Colombia, based on Rosa's testimony, Thompson's confession, and subsequent investigation. This was to Mary's benefit because Gilbert's influence was strongest in the city and not with the feds. Given the feds' strong interest in the Herman case made Gilbert a person the FBI sought to bring to justice, which also proved beneficial for Mary.

The feds made Gilbert available for a paternity test, which he passed with flying colors. And when the criminal defense partner at Adler & Stillman requested that the feds consider a plea bargain, the feds insisted that it was contingent in large part on his doing right with respect to his child support obligation to Roger, and also in terms of paying restitution to Mary for the hardships she endured due to his refusal to provide support sooner and for all the crap he put her through, not least of which being the attempted arrest he orchestrated.

Mary met with Rosa, who shared with Mary the nature of her relationship with Gilbert. This reunion bolstered Mary's resolve to achieve financial independence for herself and Roger.

Mary decided she first needed sufficient support from Gilbert to repay her outstanding debts and support Roger and her for the next five years. After that, she was willing to take her chances that once she completed her doctorate, she would become established in her profession and would be able to fully support Roger on her own.

She hashed this out with me and we also conferred with a financial adviser who had expertise in projecting child support needs. Part of the equation was also Gilbert's resources, and as part of the plea bargain negotiations, he had to submit the financial disclosure required by Family Court.

We concluded that $500,000 was the magic number to permit Mary to pay her outstanding debts and adequately take care of Roger's needs over the next five years, as well as also cover Mary's and Roger's regular living expenses and Mary's tuition costs for the final year of her doctoral work. We thought that that amount would also serve to penalize Gilbert for being such a prick.

We informed the U.S. Attorney that $500,000 was our bottom line and considering that this was much less than the amount Gilbert would have been ordered to pay to support Roger until Roger reached twenty-one, negotiations started at $1 million dollars.

We eventually settled at $750,000, plus an additional 10 percent of that amount to be paid by Gilbert for legal fees and other costs incurred by Mary. The plea bargain required that these sums be paid prior to sentencing, which they were, and Gilbert was sentenced to two years in a federal penitentiary.

Mary sought to share what she considered to be a $250,000 windfall with those who assisted her, but I made it clear to her that she and Roger alone were entitled to that and Mick backed me up in a manner that only he can do. In fact, we offered to give her the additional $75,000 awarded for fees and costs, but she insisted that it was more than fully earned by me and my team, which included Mick, Richie, and the others who helped us.

CHAPTER 27

"Makes this life worth livin'."

"**Al, that asshole** Gilbert's biggest mistake was underestimatin' you."

"What do you mean, Mick?"

"Shit, we pulled out all the fuckin' stops. We were ready for just about every possible trick he cudda thrown at us. But all he done was a Herman rerun. We lucky he don't think much of you, Al."

"Thanks loads, Mick."

Mick continued, "And now you tell me that he really ain't even have nuttin' to do with that call to the reporter."

"Yeah. I finally got hold of Peggy. They filed the Order to Show Cause with her office, so Family Court was aware of the prohibition on Mary's starting a paternity and child support action until the hearing for the Order to Show Cause."

"Okay, so what?"

"Well, Peggy, as chief clerk, saw the temporary restraining orders' confidentiality and publicity restrictions. She finally realized what I was up against with Gilbert and Stillman. So, she decided that she'd help to level the playing field by publicizing Mary's claims. Unfortunately for me, she wasn't aware of the threat the judge made at that informal conference to throw any violator in jail. She was later shocked and shamed when she learned that her call landed me in jail."

"But wait, what's the story with the phone."

"Gilbert had previously somehow found out that she was talking with me and threatened to nix her appointment to chief clerk of the Family Court if she spoke with me again. I knew she was going out of town for a funeral, but did not know that she went to Chicago. She bought the disposable phone at O'Hare and called me at home surreptitiously to let me know why she could not talk to me anymore.

"Then Theresa spotted the call from the 312 area code, which was Peg's call to me using the disposable phone on the night before that first meeting with Stillman and Gilbert. Based on that earlier call, we put two and two together and concluded that Peg used the same phone to call the reporter. We naturally assumed it was at Gilbert's request, but now we know it was Peggy trying to help me."

"That may be, but why the fuck did she go down the slide of slime and become his whore?"

"All I could say is that she never was the best judge of men. That was the case going back to our law school days. Now, don't forget that even Mary found that Gilbert can be quite charming—so did Rosa, for that matter. Peg said that prior to the conference they had gone out for dinner and he was quite flirtatious, but that the nature of their relationship changed during their time together at that conference in Philly, where she said he swept her off her feet. And Peg also admitted to the implied job security that accompanied this change in relationship—and don't forget she gave up a practice that took her years to establish and which would take that much more effort to reestablish now at her age—and being on his good side strengthened the potential for an eventual judgeship appointment, her ultimate dream."

"She's real screwy if you ask me. What a fucked-up price to pay."

"You are a thousand percent right, Mick. It was absolutely short-sighted for her to go down that road. Thankfully, with Gilbert gone, she'll be judged according to her abilities. The appropriate ones, of course."

"Don't look at me. I ain't no sexist. Anyways, what I come to talk to you about, Al, is I think we need to celebrate Mary's whompin' of Gilbert."

"You read my mind, Mick. We put together quite a team to pull this thing off and we've got to bring everyone together to celebrate and tell them how appreciative we are of their contributions."

"Great to hear there are some things we agree on."

"Mick, don't start. I acknowledged how wrong my doubts were about you and how this victory would not have been possible without you. So, you know how grateful I am and, going forward, I will be that much more eager for your advice."

"I'm shocked and honored. *Gracie.*

"Anyways, I already talked to John over at Mama Maria's, and that'll be a good place to have this celebration."

"Agreed."

"I'll call around and get it set up."

"Thanks, Mick."

◆

AND SO, ONE weekend night at the truly fabulous Mama Maria's restaurant, the following cast of characters is assembled: me, Mick, Richie Abbatello, Sammy, Francesca, John Zachs, Malcolm, Vernon Daniels, Pedro Ramos, Paolo Ruiz, JBJ, Smitty, Rosa, Jose, Molly, and, of course, Mary and Roger. The FBI agents and Chief Court Officer Nelson declined our invitation. They wanted to avoid the appearance of favoritism, but expressed their gratitude that we thought of them and appreciated their efforts.

We had cocktails first so the disparate group could mingle. While the group very much worked like an orchestral team directed by Mick and me, many had never met each other.

After some antipasto, while we awaited the main course, I give a little speech thanking each member of this great collaborative effort. My highest praise is for Mick, of course. The only criticism I level is directed at yours truly for doubting Mick's abilities and judgment at the start. I acknowledge the resources that Mick brought to bear, especially allies like Malcolm and Pedro and the forward-thinking alliances that Mick had forged. I praise each person because none of them had anything to gain by contributing, but gave to the best of their abilities nevertheless. I note Mick's brilliance in tapping Smitty and JBJ, who were our eyes and ears behind enemy lines. I make particular note of the assistance rendered by JBJ, our "secret weapon," who, though previously untested, proved to be particularly reliable and helpful. JBJ blushes. (His mother would tell Mick later how much this adventure had matured this formerly apathetic fellow. And JBJ would tell me later that evening that this was the first time that anyone had believed in him.)

After I finish, Mary gets up.

Scanning the table, she starts, "I don't know where to begin, except to say how remarkable it is what you all accomplished for Roger and me. We are forever in your debt and we'll never forget each one of you and what you did for us.

"I could not have imagined that things would turn out the way they did.

"I know Al from our time together at Gilbert's firm. He was the nicest person there. An honest, humble, capable attorney. I knew he would not turn me down, no matter that he knew little about family law. I was so desperate, I had to do whatever I had to do. I just had to fight for my baby.

"Al told me how tough the odds were. We were up against such a big firm with super talent and great resources. Al was very honest when he went through the pros and cons of my case, promising nothing except that he would try his best. But I knew he would do his best and I was confident that somehow he would find a way.

"So, while Al, like any good attorney, made me aware of the potential pitfalls, along comes Mick, so brash, super confident, amazingly resourceful. So very sure of himself. Mick's confidence removed many of my doubts and made me strong, especially during those times when things looked bleak, like when Al was thrown in jail and when I knew I had to go through my own arrest, even though I knew it was staged.

"But together Al and Mick did it. Now, don't think I forgot about the serious disagreements they had when this started, but they were soon on the same page and worked together so well. And when I say 'together' that includes each and every one of you. I know Al and Mick agree that they could not have done it without you. Each of you made a critical contribution, provided a key piece to the puzzle that made it possible for Roger and me to achieve justice and get the support that will give us a good life.

"Our eyes were opened to the possibilities that happen when people come together and lend their unique talents to accomplish a goal.

"Roger and I cannot thank each one of you enough. We pledge you our support in any way we can to help you in your time of need. May God bless you all and may we all learn from this great adventure."

Mary bows and then takes Roger by the hand and together they approach each person around the table to share kisses, embraces, and a few words of heartfelt thanks and appreciation.

Later, during dessert and coffee Mick takes the floor.

"Listen, I agree with all that my cousin Al and my friend Mary said to all youse. But I can't agree with what Al says about hisself. We wouldn't be here today if he ain't said yes to Mary when she come to him for help. And my cousin Al here says yes when he knew he had a major battle ahead and that it cudda been a losin' battle. Ain't no way the odds in his favor. He was up against a slimy, tricky mother and a high-powered law firm. Any doubts he had about me I can't say were wrong. He ain't wanted nobody to interfere with what he hadda do to help Mary. At the time, he honestly thought that I'd've (Mary, please hold little Roger's ears) fuck everything up. I once was a thug. Al don't know how much a thug I still was and he was afraid. He ain't lookin' for no credit for hisself. No way! No, he was scared I'd screw things up for Mary. So, his worry was legit.

"I'm at fault for not helpin' him gain the confidence he needed to trust me. I cudda been a little humble, but I came on strong 'cause I knew I could help. I shudda thought more about where his head was at. But to his great credit, once we got goin', we—youse, he, me—kicked ass and got the job done, and done real good for Mary and Roger.

"Now youse all know about the money that that dirt bag Gilbert hadda pay. It included a nice piece of change for legal and other expenses, which we wanted Mary to keep, but she says we oughta spread it to each of us, to cover costs and to show her thanks. Well, Al and me went down the line to each and every one of youse, and all of youse said, 'No, use my share to help somebody else.' Al, who's owed the most for the legal work he done, was the first to say this. Anyways, we gonna put the 75 Gs I'm talkin' about into Al's escrow account and it's gonna be used to help folks in need. And decisions about how that money is gonna be spent is gonna be made by a committee—of Al, Rich, Malcolm, Pedro, and me. We'll see where this thing goes and adjust, if necessary. That gotta depend, of course, on how fast this money gets spent. But we'll see what happens and we'll report back all about it, since each one of youse are contributors to this here fund and have a right to know.

"As we wrap this up, I gotta tell youse about the great feelin' I got for all of youse and for what we done did together. This kinda thing and the feelin' it brings to me is one of the very few things that makes this life worth livin'. You know, we got all this pain, when people ain't treated right, 'cause of the terrible things we do to each other and that happens to folks, but there are some few things that make you happy to be alive to experience 'em, a few very special things.

"Lots of times I bitch about people who think they know everything 'cause of their high falutin' education. Lots of times I talk about my havin' one of 'em doctorates too, one from the university of the streets. Of course, this ain't mean I know everything or that I ain't never made no mistakes. Just ask the poor ladies who got stuck with me for any period of time. But anyways, I been thinkin' about when people talk about 'our kind', and I wrote down some things and I hope this ain't gonna bore the shit outa any of youse.

"Here's what I wrote down:

"Our kind. Who the fuck's our kind?

"Take Italians, for example. You have Napolitano, Abbruzzese, Barese, Siciliano. You go north of Rome and my mother says you got either Swiss or French or German!

"And whoever our kind is, we're outnumbered.

"Whatever power we got and wanna keep, ain't no way we gonna hold it, unless we fight off everybody—and while firepower will do the trick for a short time, eventually we gonna be overpowered and outnumbered.

"For survival, we gotta have allies and alliances with those who ain't our kind, who are our friends 'cause of things we got in common, like things that are important to both of us, that becomes mutual respect too, as time goes by.

"Face the facts, those who ain't our kind ain't gonna go away. Even a big ass effort to get rid of those who ain't our kind only works for a short time. Remember that dick Hitler and his asshole Nazis and what happened to 'em. After a while they were defeated and put to shame.

"We hear of some 'our kinds' causing commotion every so often, even these days, even after all we shudda learned. All 'our kinds' that act up are gonna get defeated and lose after a while. No doubt about it.

"Thanks a lot for listenin' to this, but thanks mostly for showin' that there ain't but only one kind, and that's *humankind* and youse all showed how we can all get along and help each other. And for that we oughta all be proud and thankful to one another.

"Now, as they said in Vernon's church when I visited one Sunday: Can I get an amen?"

Everyone stands up and shouts their amens as loud as they can, and then everyone hugs and kisses and slaps each other on the back in grateful appreciation for what we accomplished together and for the great lessons that we learned.

Acknowledgments

To ACCOMPLISH ANYTHING worthwhile, one always needs a little help from his/her friends (or acquaintances—and in some cases, kind strangers).

Those responsible, directly and indirectly, in rendering meaningful assistance to me that resulted in the finished product that this book represents are too numerous to mention (or even remember). To those not mentioned, if you know who you are, please forgive me.

But, nonetheless, I must make special mention of the following:

He will surely be surprised for being singled out, but I owe a debt of gratitude to my buddy (and college classmate and former law client) Peter Bourbeau for getting me back to reading. Pete would always talk about what and who he read and encourage me to read this or that book. It was he who introduced me to two of my favorite contemporary writers, Dennis Lehane and George Pelecanos. For me, reading led to writing and it was Pete who got me going.

I will expound upon how this story was originally conceived more than 20 years ago in the backstory section of this series's website, www.AlandMickForte.net.

Nevertheless, I returned to the dormant story for material to complete the assignments for an on-line writing course I took at the end of 2016. The course was through The Center for Fiction (centerforfiction.org) here in New

York City. Writer extraordinaire Jason Starr (jasonstarr. com) taught the course, and I am indebted to Jason for getting me back into the story, and for his positive feedback and encouragement, which got me off my duff to pick up from where I had left off.

I must also thank distinguished playwright and the 2016 winner of The Center for Fiction's first novel award (for *The Castle Cross the Magnet Carter*—a must read, BTW), Kia Corthron (http://www.kiacorthron-author. com/), for reading a draft of a portion of this book. The encouragement from someone of Kia's stature was another significant motivator for me to finish writing this book.

I am immensely indebted to my fabulous editor, Linda Hetzer, who provided detailed and meticulous editorial guidance. Linda herself is a writer, editor, and speaker. She is the author of *Moving On: A Practical Guide to Downsizing the Family Home*, about getting rid of stuff and keeping the memories. There will be more about Linda in the website. I must publicly thank Linda's daughter, Elizabeth Ginsberg, a former work colleague, for informing me that her mom is an editor. The rest is history and this book.

As diligent an editor as Linda is, she had trouble verifying the spelling of the Italian expressions sprinkled throughout this book. I had failed to inform Linda that those were not "mainstream" Italian words, but sayings in the peculiar Neapolitan dialect. To check those expressions' spelling, I enlisted my sister, Sister Antonina Avitabile, MSC. Toni was reluctant at first, reminding me how vulgar and sexual those expressions are. She overcame her reluctance when I reminded her that every single one of those expressions came out of our saintly—albeit also earthy—mother's mouth. Thanks, Toni. And *grazie*, Mama, Francesca Cuomo Avitabile, who for some still mysterious reason left the idyllic isle of Ischia at the age of 21 to come to South Brooklyn in 1947.

Finally, I must acknowledge 1106 Design, its Brooklyn-born leader Michele DeFilippo and Ronda Rawlins and Carol Herschberg for assisting me to "self-publish" this book. In truth, "self-publish" when you work with Michele et al is a misnomer, as I had no clue how to get this book published and all credit on that front belongs to 1106 Design.

About the Author

LIKE HIS CHARACTERS Al and Mick Forte, Alex S. Avitabile grew up back in the day (i.e., the '50s and '60s) on the then "mean streets" of South Brooklyn—present day Carroll Gardens. For the past some thirty years he has lived within walking distance of his original "hood," which is now less mean and more gentrified, about which Alex is not so sure that's a good thing.

Alex retired after practicing law for thirty-four years, and *Occupational Hazard* is his first published work of fiction. Alex is presently working on the second installment of the Al/Mick Forte series, which he hopes to publish in 2019.

Go to www.AlandMickForte.net, the website for the Al and Mick Forte Series, to read more about Alex.

Hard Soul Brooklyn tee shirts are available from:
www.hardsoulboutique.com

Made in the USA
San Bernardino, CA
25 October 2018